Wings of the Golden Dragon

AIRSHIP 27 PRODUCTIONS

Wings of the Golden Dragon
© 2016 Barbara Doran

Published by Airship 27 Productions
www.airship27.com
www.airship27hangar.com

Interior illustrations © 2016 Gary Kato
Cover illustration © 2016 Rob Davis

Editor: Ron Fortier
Associate Editor: Gordon Dymowski
Marketing and Promotions Manager: Michael Vance
Production and design by Rob Davis.

ISBN-10: 1-946183-04-0
ISBN-13: 978-1-946183-04-0

Printed in the United States of America

10 9 8 7 6 5 4 3 2 1

Wings of the Golden Dragon

By Barbara Doran

Foreward

Shanghai in the 1930s was a turbulent, exciting and dangerous time. Not for nothing was it known as the New York of the East, combining as it did High Society, criminal lowlifes, businessmen seeking their fortunes and dozens of foreign powers all vying for supremacy in Asia. At the time of the story, while Japan and China had clashed over the city once, the European population was still convinced that they would prosper.

Much of this story would not be possible without the dedicated work of historian Harriet Sergeant and a marvelous reprint of the very travel guide Conall carries with him throughout the book. I offer my heartfelt thanks for both books and suggest them for any historian interested in the subject of pre-World War II China.

It was impossible to bring in every last detail of life in Shanghai. Such a work would require several volumes of stories and a cast of thousands. As it is, the cast of "Wings of the Golden Dragon" is so varied that a list seems in order. What follows does not include every character who appears in the book, but I hope it provides a sufficient cast list to give a good idea of who is who and what is what.

Owing to some characters being named by American convention and some by Asian (last name first), I divide the list accordingly. Also, I've tended to follow the old Wade-Giles system for transliterating Chinese names and words. My apologies to those more accustomed to the modern Pinyin, but I felt it was more in keeping with the tone of the era.

American & European Cast:

Cheh Chang: A Chinese-American businessman from Strikersport, Cheh Chang is the owner of Jeen Loon Shipping. Rumored to have criminal connections all over the world and to be the boss of a secret society, Cheh has come to Shanghai to deal with his errant daughter.

Mudan Chang: The only daughter of Cheh Chang, the Boss of Strikersport's Chinatown. Born in America, she has been raised to honor her father and obey him, even though her heart would have her go with Conall McLeod. She has been taught martial arts from childhood and is considered one of the best fighters of her extended family. She has come to Shanghai against her father's wishes to protect Conall.

Sir Bruce Franer: A British Knight, he was the first member of the consortium to be contacted by Soong Kou. He seems more interested in horses, however, leaving Murtagh to worry over the delay in examining the engine.

Major Grant-Merchant: A British officer assigned to Shanghai, the major has learned a little of the conspiracy surrounding a mysterious new engine and is attempting to discover more about the situation. He suspects Mudan Chang of being deeply involved owing to her father's rumored involvement with both the tongs and triads.

Lord William Holm: Another member of the consortium, Lord William also seems uninterested in completing the bargain and far more interested in what his mistress, Fukushima Hikaru has to say.

Conall McLeod: An American from Strikersport, Conall is a highly skilled engineer whose skills have been called upon to investigate a new engine for his employer, Peter Striker and the British-Oriental Consortium run by Sir Bruce Franer. He is in love with Mudan Chang, despite California law preventing their getting married.

James Murtagh: A British merchant with the consortium, Murtagh is mostly interested in only one thing; money. He is impatiently waiting to find out if the engine Soong Kou is offering is of any use.

Peter Striker: An American businessman from Strikersport, Striker was brought into the consortium by Murtagh in hopes of getting the other members moving. So far the best he's managed to do is call Conall in to examine the engine.

Chinese Cast:

Chen Tang: Also known as the Black Jade Fox, Chen Tang is a wandering adventurer known best for his talent for thievery and knife work. Being a lazy sort, it takes a bit to get him going and when he does move, it's generally to his own benefit.

Feng Wugong: A member of the Soong Gang, Feng has been assigned the task of capturing Conall and keeping him from revealing the true nature of the engine Conall is to investigate. He is a skilled sorcerer who summons poisonous insects to do his bidding.

Feng Zhanchi: Wugong's brother, Zhanchi is a pilot with the Chinese National Aviation Corporation. He's been hired by James Murtagh, a member of the British-Oriental Consortium, to fly whatever plane is fitted with the engine the consortium is buying. As the plane has yet to be built, he has been regulated to a chauffer's duty, much to his annoyance.

Soong Kou: The boss of the Soong gang, he and his lieutenant stole a powerful device from Khaitan and have been attempting to turn it to use in an engine with varying degrees of success.

Zhao Zhi Lin: The daughter of a local Warlord, Zhi Lin has been hired to assist in capturing Conall. A talented chef, she is also skilled in the use of herbs and drugs for other, more nefarious purposes.

Zhao Zhu: The Warlord of Chinglung Mountain, Zhao seeks to capture the device to further his own aim of becoming China's next Emperor.

Japanese Cast:

Fukushima Hikaru: A Japanese woman of unknown background, Hikaru is ostensibly the mistress of Lord William Holm, yet another member of the British-Oriental Consortium.

Kurumata Katashi: A member of the Japanese Navy, Katashi has been ordered to capture the engine the Soong Gang is offering. He is young, somewhat impetuous, and furious at having been relegated to Shanghai after the destruction of his last assignment at Tōgō base. (Author Note: Tōgō base was the predecessor of the infamous Unit 731.)

Shikawa Nori: Ostensibly a Captain of the Japanese Navy, Shikawa runs a small spy operation in Shanghai. Having learned of the Soong engine, he is interested in capturing it for Japan. Given, of course, it really works as claimed.

Supernatural Cast:

Bai She: A visitor from the ancient kingdom of Khaitan, Bai She has been sent to retrieve an item stolen from his land. Although blind, he is a minor deity in Khaitan, with the power to transform to a great white serpent. He is accompanied by his familiars, a group of eight shadows who aid him in his search.

Shen: Although ostensibly a chauffer, Shen is Bai She's compatriot and is assisting him in rescuing the device Soong has stolen. Shen is a minor deity of Khaitan's dragon clan and given the proper recognition, has the power to transform to a great purple dragon.

Raud: A dragon from Britain, he has been part of Shanghai's criminal underworld ever since it was ceded to the English in the 1800s.

Chapter One
The Other Side of The World

The scent of the sea breeze was changing. What had been brisk, clear and sharp with salt was now faintly tinged with the familiar odor of fish. Conall McLeod looked up from his guidebook, relieved. There'd been little to do aboard the *Empress of the China Sea* but read and he'd been discouraged from bringing along his manuals. He was, after all, supposedly on vacation.

Supposedly being the story he was to tell any who asked. Fortunately, no one aboard the *Empress* had been interested. The crew was too busy with their duties to worry over a young American on his first trip abroad. As for the passengers, most were far more interested in being entertained than in making the acquaintance of a poorly dressed, gangly, red-head just barely out of his teens.

Not that Conall minded the disregard. His only regret was the lack of stimulatiing reading material in the ship's library. The only thing he'd found of interest had been a guidebook of Shanghai, "All About Shanghai and Environs (1935 Edition)", and even that had soporific qualities to it. When, of course, it wasn't infuriatingly vague, full of excited commentary that said very little with far too many words.

Going to the rail surrounding the upper deck, Conall saw the first signs of the Yangtze River. The guidebook had been right in that much, he reflected. Water that had been a dark deep green was lightening as they drew closer and closer to the Yangtze delta. If he remembered correctly, that meant there'd be a pilot boarding soon to guide the steamer the rest of the way to Shanghai.

As if to prove him right, the ship began to slow as a smaller boat approached the *Empress* from the north. Soon after, the ship came to a complete halt and he heard the sound of men speaking in Chinese. Having learned a bit of the language back in Strikersport's Chinatown, he recognized a few choice curses in there.

Those curses made him frown. He would freely admit to being easily distracted, paying attention to things most people ignored, but he was not so oblivious as to miss tones of fear and anger, even when phrased in a language he'd barely learned.

Curious, Conall made his way towards the commotion, sticking his guidebook in his pocket and whistling as he walked, pretending to be simply taking the air. If there was trouble he'd go for help but he had to be sure, first. He'd hate to make a fool of himself crying wolf.

As Conall drew closer he quickly realized the commotion on the deck below was more than he could take on by himself. He was stronger than his skinny frame appeared, being accustomed to handling the tools of his trade and keeping unruly workers in line, but he couldn't fight so many. Already the small group of boarders, dressed in black, their faces covered with white handkerchiefs, had overpowered the few sailors who'd met them at the ladder. He could see them just behind the steps leading down to the lower deck.

The sound of Conall's whistle had the hoped for effect of pausing the invasion. The attackers went quiet, evading attention. He continued along the rail, catching a glimpse—here and there—of dark-clad figures shoving limp bodies out of sight on the deck below.

Deciding he'd seen enough to justify sounding the alarm, Conall put his hands in his pockets and muttered, "Now what did I do with my pipe? Must have left it in my room." He turned around, intending to saunter quickly back, a man on an obvious mission, when he spotted the centipede crawling its way towards him.

It was huge, easily as long as his forearm and bigger than his two thumbs in width, and it moved with obvious purpose. Not liking the look of it, Conall moved just as fast, slamming his foot down just barely in time to crush it beneath the sole of his boot. The sound of its shell crunching was almost as unpleasant as the realization that it was still alive. He could feel it moving, trying to crawl out from under his foot. He stepped harder.

"You saw it."

The voice that interrupted Conall's attempt to squash the centipede had an English accent. When he looked up he found a Chinese man standing in front of him. Dressed in a long dark-red robe and loose trousers of black silk, the man's face had a hard, self-composed, quality that suggested he was accustomed to giving commands and being obeyed.

Again the man said, "You saw it."

"What do you mean?" Conall asked, as a half-dozen more centipedes came crawling out from the stranger's long sleeves. With a toss, the man flung the things at Conall, who automatically leapt backwards. Now the centipede he'd stepped on was part of the attack and he felt something bite his ankle before he could get away.

A wave of dizziness came over Conall and he stumbled, trying to brush the centipedes away and feeling another bite as he struggled. Now he was close to blacking out, the creatures' poison working its way into his system.

Something moved behind him, caught him by the arm and gently lowered him to the floor. "Stay quiet," a familiar voice said in his ear. "I will not let them hurt you."

As he leaned against the wall beside him, eyes wide and vision blurred, Conall stared at the newcomer. He knew her despite the western makeup and the blond hair with its elaborate and elegant curls. He'd seen her from a distance earlier and thought she'd seemed familiar. Now, up close, he'd recognize those sternly beautiful features anywhere. They belonged to Mudan Chang, the beloved and only child of Strikersport's richest Chinese businessman, Cheh Chang. She was also the woman Conall was determined to marry; given California law ever allowed him to do so.

《《《

Mudan rose to face the sorcerer who had attacked Conall. She had to force all thought from her mind of Conall's expression when he'd recognized her. His face was suffused with pain, confusion and fear, all combined with a yearning to be the one protecting instead of the one protected. All part of the tie between them that a year's separation could not shatter. Forbidden to speak, forbidden to meet and forbidden to love, she'd obeyed her father in only two of those things. Seeing him hurt made her hurt in turn. It also made her furious.

Looking on the stranger, Mudan spotted signs of at least a half-dozen hidden blades; the fan, the toes of his shoes, his belt and quite probably his arm band. Indeed, the only thing he wore that didn't appear to be a weapon was the silvery dragon bracelet that curled around his left wrist. He watched her silently, using his fan with an insouciant and arrogant air.

Slowly Mudan asked in English, "What poison have you used on this man?" It was impolite; a direct approach no native-born Chinese would ever take. Born in America, of a family considered the lowest of the low, Mudan felt no need to follow those old traditions. Especially not with a man whose attack might have killed the man she loved.

"Who are you that asks and why would you know?" The stranger had recalled his centipedes, already used to chill effect on those sailors on the deck below. Mudan didn't doubt he'd summon them again and was already contemplating how to counter their attack. She settled into stance and hoped her skirt wouldn't get in the way.

Mudan said quietly, "I do not give my name to one who does not offer his own. As for why I would know? The man is one my father values for his skills. I will not permit him to be harmed."

The stranger drew out a fan, spinning it on his forefinger as if to distract Mudan. "Your father? What low-born, illiterate, dung-raking tortoise spawned a flower like yourself? Perhaps he will sell you to me? There are houses that pay well for white girls."

Recognizing distraction when she heard it, Mudan dropped down below the grasping hands of the man who'd been sneaking up behind her. She spun round, taking her attacker down with a leg sweep and elbowed him in the face before somersaulting around to evade another attack. All while keeping aware of the sorcerer as she took a moment to slip her jacket off so she could move more freely.

Three more men attacked then, forcing Mudan to spin and leap in a series of rapid evasions, her skirt tearing in the process. At the same time she struck as fast and hard as she could, cracking jaws and twisting arms to the breaking point. Her attackers were good but they were not her match and they quickly realized it, backing away when she kicked one over the railing and into the water below.

Their leader came at her then and he was a true challenge, not least because his style was similar to hers. Spinning low kicks that would sweep the unwary off their feet, rapid hand strikes that could easily break whatever they touched. He was good, far better than the others, but he seemed oddly weak. That made her suspicious and she watched him, catching brief flashes of real skill.

Deliberately, Mudan faltered, so her enemy became sure he was winning. She could see Conall struggling, wanting to help her and hoped he'd realize he couldn't. She skidded along the deck and hit the railing, allowing herself to spin over the rail. Gripping tight, she swung— seemingly helpless—over the deck below.

The stranger was on her a moment later, grabbing for the top of her head so he could drive his fan—its blade now revealed—into her face. That had been exactly what she'd waited for and she made her move, raising her legs and hooking her knees around the nearest post just before catching hold of his one hand with both hers. Without hesitation, she flung herself backwards, dragging him over the edge with her by the weight of her body.

He clung tight, swinging around wildly while she held his wrist. "I'll tear your scalp from your head," he hissed furiously.

"Small loss," she told him in return, swinging along with him. With luck she could drop him into the ocean instead of the deck below. She was about to release his arm when a voice spoke inside her head. It was a still, small, voice but it was one she knew well and one she could not disobey. Immediately, she slid her fingers around her enemy's dragon bracelet. "Come child," the other voice whispered through her, the feverish heat of His touch making her shudder. As she let her enemy fall, the bracelet alone remained.

The stranger yelled furiously as he dropped, still clutching her blond wig and narrowly missing the lower deck. The splash he made as he landed in the water was more than satisfying.

⟨⟨⟨

Feng Wugong cursed and flailed as he struggled for the boat he and his men had used to reach the *Empress of the China Sea*. His fight with that little brat had taken too long and allowed the crew of the *Empress* to realize they were under attack. His entire plan had depended on getting aboard and capturing their target quickly. That was now impossible. The *Empress's* crew would surely be on guard the rest of the way to Shanghai.

"Do you plan on keeping that wig for a souvenir?"

Wugong glared at the speaker leaning over the railing of the boat. The skinny little Northerner calling himself Chen Tang was annoyingly quick with his tongue and unhesitant with his mockery. No one, not even the much feared Big-eared Du, nor even Pockmarked Huang was safe. It was as if the fellow thought himself immortal. Certainly it sometimes seemed he were given how often he survived situations that left others tattered corpses for the rats.

Without a word, Wugong hoisted himself up the rope one of his men lowered for him and threw the wig at Chen. The man caught it easily and examined it. "Pretty," he commented. "And expensive." He shoved it into a pocket, seemingly unconcerned by the way it soaked and distended the fine silk fabric of his jacket.

Wugong ignored the man long enough to order his boat to get away from the *Empress*. Now that they'd failed their mission staying would be the worst sort of dangerous. Only when he was satisfied they'd escaped did he turn back to Chen to demand, "Why the hell didn't you come and help?"

Chen shrugged off the question, sweeping his black bangs away from his broad forehead with a jerk of his head. "Two reasons. One, you told me you could handle the targets without me. Two, I had one of my coughing fits. This sea air isn't good for my lungs."

"Sea water will be even worse," Wugong snarled. "I should throw you overboard."

"Do. I'll remember the favor when I reach shore again. Might take a bit of walking, but it's not that deep here, you know." Chen grinned, then eyed Wugong's arm sharply. "What happened to that bracelet of yours?"

Startled, Wugong grabbed for his wrist and realized the thing was gone. "That…." He found every curse he could regarding that little Westerner with her pretense of martial skill. "She took my Quicksilver Dragon!" It shouldn't have been possible. The magic that had bound the device to his service meant that it wouldn't leave him without a fight. Or, at least, it ought to have meant that.

"Yes. She did," Chen said eyeing the *Empress* thoughtfully, as the two ships grew more distant from each other "I wonder if it went with her intentionally, or if it just had enough of you. All things considered, I wouldn't blame it at all."

"I'll kill that white devil woman! I swear it. Whoever she is, I swear I'll kill her! She will not get away with tricking me again!" The bracelet was but a small part of a greater whole, but it was nearly impossible to control the rest without it. Besides, what if someone discovered its true nature? He'd have to find that girl and get it back.

"White devil woman?"

Wugong was close to exploding. Even if Chen had been too lazy to help, he'd obviously watched the fight from the safety of Wugong's boat. "That brat who thinks she knows something about *wusha*!" he snapped. "The one who had that wig."

"Oh. Her." Amusement suffused Chen's narrow features and he gazed towards the *Empress* thoughtfully. "She fights like my brother. All elbows and knees. But white devil woman?"

Wugong didn't know who Chen Tang's brother was, nor anything about his fighting style. Nor did he care. "I was right up next to her, you idiot. Do you think I can't tell a white westerner? She's probably an American secret agent trained in some cheap mimicry of the art."

Shrugging, Chen searched his pockets. "Well, if you say so, Wugong. Far be it for me to suggest you might be wrong."

It was possible Wugong would have lost his temper entirely with Chen at that point, but before he could say another word, Chen pulled out a soggy package of cigarettes. The look on the thief's face as he realized his insouciant gesture with the soaking wet wig earlier had backfired was ample revenge for his overly smart tongue and insults.

Chapter Two
Have Your Customs Declarations Prepared in Advance

Conall woke in his cabin with a start. He'd have thought the whole thing a dream but for two things. He could still feel the centipede bites in his ankle and wrist, and Mudan was in the room with him, talking to his employer. "Losing my wig complicates matters," she was saying. "Not just aboard ship. A white woman may travel in Shanghai more openly than a woman of Chinese descent. It would be different, perhaps, if I were born there, but…."

"I quite understand. Does this mean you'd like me to get another bodyguard for Conall?" Peter Striker sounded, as he often did, terribly bored and disdainful, but Conall had learned the businessman's air of eternal ennui hid a sharp mind and a dry humor.

That thought was lost in the realization that Mudan was there to protect him. He sat up, nearly falling out of his berth as a wave of dizziness washed over him. "Mudan!"

"Lay back down, Conall. You will hurt yourself." As always, she had a way of ordering him around that he found profoundly comforting. It was, he'd long since realized, her way of telling him she cared. He obeyed her quickly, turning his head to look at her.

She was a mess. She'd been dressed in a grey calf-length skirt and simple jacket when she'd come to his rescue. The fight had forced her to abandon the latter and rip the former half-way up her thigh. Her short straight hair, no longer hidden beneath the elaborate blond wig, was tangled and sweaty, bits of dark fluff standing up around her head. Her make-up was smeared, the soft peach colors wiped away to reveal the fine ivory of her face. She was busy removing the worst of the mess, revealing her sternly beautiful features.

"Are you hurt?" Conall demanded. He didn't see any sign of blood—hers or their attackers'—but that was meaningless. There were many other ways to damage a person and Mudan was small and delicately built. And strong, he reminded himself, remembering the way she'd kneed that one thug in the belly by flinging herself at him. Even so, "Mr. Striker, make her see the ship's doctor."

"There is no need to concern yourself," Mudan reassured him. "They were difficult, but no worse than some I have fought back home. The worst of my injuries are bruises and a wrenched muscle here and there."

Conall was about to argue but someone knocked on the door to the suite he and Striker shared. "Mr. Striker? Sir? The Captain wants to speak with you."

Striker sighed, straightening his suit and tie and setting himself in order. When he was done he looked the very picture of the richest man in Strikersport, his grey hair impeccably groomed and his narrow, beaky, features as arrogant and supercilious as they could possibly be. At Mudan's raised brow, he told her, "Always face authority with your best foot forward. At worst they won't notice and at best they may be confused into thinking you really are superior to them." Then he was gone, leaving Mudan alone with Conall.

It took them a few minutes before either found their voice. "I thought you said you'd never come near me again. That your father forbade it?" To be fair, Conall's father had forbidden their meeting as well. Even in a small city like Strikersport the white son of a prominent engineer could not expect to take up with the Chinese daughter of the local Tong leader without causing a scandal. Marrying her, illegal in California, was out of the question.

"Oh, he did. He doesn't know I'm here or he would have many things to say to myself, and to Mr. Striker." Mudan checked Conall's injuries and nodded with satisfaction. "You seem to have recovered, thanks in part to my Lord Meng Huang Shang. It was his power that purified the poison in your system."

Even having had long since learned that magic and other Gods existed, the fact still made Conall uncomfortable. To his mind magic was a cheat; a breaking of the rules that he wasn't sure was fair. As for owing his life to the Chang family's tutelary God? Especially one as chancy as a god of delirium? That was even harder to accept, especially since he knew how bound to the God Mudan was.

Still, he recognized the debt and said so. "Remind me to thank him.

And thank you for stopping that man. Now why are you here?"

Mudan took Striker's comb from where he'd left it and began untangling her hair, a silver bracelet he didn't recognize glittering around her left wrist. Her hair was shorter than Conall remembered, no doubt to accommodate that ridiculously elaborate wig. "As always, blunt to a fault," she sighed. "You're fortunate that's one of the things I love about you."

He waited for her answer, knowing she was trying to distract him, and she finally said, "You are officially going to Shanghai for a holiday. Unofficially, you're here to examine a new and powerful engine invented by a Chinese engineer."

"That's right," Conall agreed. The engine was being sold to The British-Oriental Consortium, but Striker had been offered a part in the company. Being a canny old bird, Striker had insisted on hiring Conall to make sure the engine—supposedly the fastest and most silent airplane engine in the world—was real. "You're here to protect me, then? But why? And why you?"

"You need protection because Mr. Striker is concerned that this is part of an elaborate scam and that anyone set to investigating the engine will either be killed or forced to pretend the engine works as claimed." Mudan answered as she cleaned off the last of her smeared makeup. "As for why me? You mean aside from the fact that I have the skills and knowledge to keep you safe in Shanghai, despite being born and bred in America?"

"Yes." Conall had never seen Mudan fight before, though her father's men had warned him she was terrifyingly fast and good. They'd been right. He'd boxed with the son of one of his father's friends for years and he suspected Mudan was faster and harder than George Jarvis could ever be. Given the right reason and need, she could kill without blinking an eye. "Aside from that."

Mudan looked at him and smiled that serene distant smile of hers. "Because you are in danger and I will have you safe."

To tell the truth, there really wasn't anything Conall could say to counter that statement, so he didn't try.

(((

The aftermath of the fight required Mr. Striker to speak quickly and eloquently in Mudan's defense. Had the *Empress* been owned by the Japanese or the British, persuading the Captain that her disguise as a white woman had been necessary might have been more difficult. Fortunately, the *Empress* belonged to a San Francisco based company whose ownership

Mudan suspected to be closer to home than her father would ever admit. Jeen Loon Enterprises had its fingers in a wide variety of pies.

If that were true, then Mudan had no hope of remaining anonymous. All she could do was pray no one would send word to her father of her whereabouts. She was supposed to be in Massachusetts studying business at Radcliffe. He wouldn't be pleased to learn that she'd agreed to this insane venture, especially given the reason.

In the end, the judicious application of gold, as Striker put it, smoothed even the roughest path and Mudan was allowed to return to her room across from Conall and Striker. It helped that her passport had her real name along with her English name of Sonya. It didn't make those who felt deceived by her pretense at whiteness any more accepting but the ship was almost to Shanghai and Mudan wasn't aboard to make friends.

The *Empress* having arrived at Whangpoo river's mouth late in the afternoon, the decision was made to wait for morning before navigating the shoals and shallow waters to Shanghai's port. By mid-morning the next day they glided past the beautifully designed and decorated buildings of the Bund, the great long street that curved alongside the river and was a newcomer's first view of a place some thought of as the New York City of China.

Having been to Shanghai as a child, Mudan knew the façade for what it was. Behind the Bund were smaller buildings. Shops and homes, some built in the western style, others older and more traditional—especially in the Chinese city. As for Chapei, to the north, the 1932 bombing had left it devastated. Her father, who'd visited since then, had told her they were still, slowly, recovering from the damage.

The ship drew into port just in time for the noon cannon to set everyone's ears ringing. Typical of Conall, though, he cocked his head and said, "Sounds to me like it could do with some repair work." They were all three standing at the rail like any tourist, staring bemusedly at the sight of the scores of rickshaws, jogging down the street and narrowly avoiding horses, carriages and motor vehicles.

"You are here for other reasons," Mudan told him. "Entertainment, for one."

"Fixing their cannon would be entertainment," Conall countered, much to Striker's amusement. Mudan gazed silently at the chill November sky and wondered what it was about her man that made him so focused on such matters.

It wasn't long after that they went through customs, which led to the all too expected discussion of why Mudan, a Chinese woman, was traveling with two white men. Mudan had expected the reaction and was inured to it. She had to put a hand on Conall's wrist to calm him, however, when the old man in charge of examining her luggage rudely demanded to know where she'd gotten her bracelet.

"It is a gift," Mudan told him, delicately sliding her foot over Conall's toes to keep him from interrupting. "From one who loves me." That was true in a sense. It was, after all, her God's will she take the thing, although she had not yet guessed why. Meng Huang Shang's love could bring great trouble on its recipient, but was often worth it in the end.

Mr. Striker smiled and murmured something incomprehensible in a tone that suggested her statement pleased him. That, along with the bribe he slid into the custom agent's hands at the appropriate moment, got them through the rest of the custom checks with most of Mudan's dignity intact. It was obvious from the custom man's manner that he thought she was with Striker as his mistress. It would have annoyed her less if they'd made that assumption about herself and Conall, but it seemed her love's talent for appearing ineffectual and distracted created an impression, and not a very good one.

"It's just as well your disguise was ruined," Striker told Mudan once they were alone. "It was one thing having you give the impression you were white aboard ship, as it allowed you to stay closer to McLeod without drawing attention to yourself. But it'd be a difficult pretense to keep up, here in Shanghai. Easier, I think, to have it assumed you've attached yourself to us for obvious reasons."

"You may be right," she agreed, ignoring Conall's protest at the idea of anyone assuming she was Striker's—or even Conall's—mistress. "Will Sir Bruce accept my presence?"

"Sir Bruce is oblivious to anything that doesn't have four legs and jump over gates. As for the others, they'll simply assume you're with me," Striker answered, hailing a cab, much to Mudan's relief. Rickshaws were uncomfortable in many ways; not least in the feeling of distaste it gave her to treat a human being like a beast of burden. That they always jostled her in ways she didn't care for didn't help.

A beautifully maintained silver and green car with a flowery pattern on its door pulled up and its driver jumped out to assist them into the back. He was well-kept and almost too handsome; with arrogant features that reminded Mudan of one of the statues of the Eight Immortals her father displayed back home. She couldn't help noticing his hair was long enough to pull into a smooth black ponytail, tied at the nape of his neck.

Once settled, Conall made his opinion clear. "Mudan isn't that sort of woman."

"I'm well aware of that," Striker answered, smiling. "But allowing folk to think she is doesn't make her one, nor does it require her to behave as one. It simply makes things easier socially. Shanghailanders are… pigheaded and boorish enough to look upon the Chinese as simple-minded animals in need of intelligent guidance, preferably by Great Britain."

"You never told me I was going to need protection," Conall pointed out. "Nor did you mention that the woman I love would be protecting me. At least allow me the dignity of complaining when I find out what that means for her."

Mudan was touched, understanding why Conall felt that way. She was also concerned, because she'd just noticed they were being followed by a large black limousine. It'd been behind them for several blocks now and its driver strongly resembled the man who'd attacked the *Empress* the afternoon before.

⟨⟨⟨

Feng Zhanchi watched the cab ahead of them sourly. So that was the American engineer Striker had hired to examine the new engine. This McLeod didn't look nearly bright enough to understand how a wheel turned on an axle, much less how a combustion engine worked. Admittedly, Zhanchi didn't understand how the thing worked either, but he was a pilot, not an engineer. He knew enough to repair any obvious damage but not enough to know why the new engine was so fast and so efficient.

Zhanchi's greatest concern was the sheer number of foreigners involved in what—to his mind—ought to be purely a Chinese concern. It was bad enough that the China National Aviation Corporation was practically run by its American partners. Even worse when the British, arrogant bastards that they were, tried to stick their fingers into the pot. Still, money was all too often short and the CNAC had lost a good plane and a decent pilot half a year earlier. Gast had been too sure of himself when it came to the dangers of China's coastline, but he didn't deserve being lost in the China Sea.

"Follow them," the man in the back seat of the car said calmly. James Murtagh was a senior partner in the consortium. He'd commandeered Zhanchi as his driver, on the assumption that since the CNAC had plenty of pilots, Zhanchi was in need of something to do. That doing so took him out of the rotation entirely and meant Zhanchi couldn't get so much as one of the few flights they allowed him was not Murtagh's concern.

To Zhanchi's surprise, following the cab became more difficult than usual, even in Shanghai's traffic. One always had to be careful. Rickshaw drivers could be unpredictable and recklessly indifferent to danger; to themselves, to their customers and to those around them. There were horses and carriages and cars belonging to foreigners who'd yet to learn how to drive in Shanghai, all getting in the way and confusing themselves and everyone else. Then there were the long, elegant sedans with their inevitable contingent of heavily armed Russians. One didn't upset those sorts casually, whether they protected a rich man or a gangster.

Given that, the cab carrying the Americans seemed to be on a suicide mission. It kept changing lanes, turning onto narrow streets that were just barely wide enough for it to pass and all the while going too fast for Shanghai's mid-afternoon traffic.

Zhanchi was up to the challenge and he slid between carts, carriages, cars and people without hesitation. If that cab driver wanted to play he'd give them a game to remember. Behind him, Murtagh cursed, pushed sideways in his seat by the force of one turn. "Be careful!"

"You said follow. I follow," Zhanchi answered, using the most cheerful and foolish tone he could. He didn't care if the Americans got away. It wouldn't matter if they did, because there'd be a meeting sooner or later, but he was perfectly happy to inconvenience Murtagh by a far too literal interpretation of his orders.

One turn sent a food cart rolling into another, leaving a wake of tipped over vegetables and fruits, along with angry shouts. Another took them into the old city and resulted in more shouting, accompanied by thrown produce when the chase came close to bringing down a half dozen old men out walking their sparrows. The American's cab did have the sense to slow down at least, so while they were in danger of being mobbed by annoyed townsfolk they weren't likely to run anyone over.

Slowing down had another effect. Murtagh, who'd been too busy trying to stay upright to do more than complain, had had quite enough by this time. He grabbed Zhanchi by the shoulder and ordered fiercely, "Stop!"

"They will get away," Zhanchi said stubbornly. "I will speed up."

"No! Damn your eyes, boy. You'll get us killed."

Zhanchi realized his boss was closer to right than he knew. The cab was slowing to a halt ahead of them, not because it had given up, nor because its driver thought they were safe. No, it was stopping because it couldn't go any further, there being a wall and about twenty men blocking their path, all looking more than ready to show the foreign devils why it wasn't a good idea to go wandering around Shanghai's less savory neighborhoods.

"*Ahmitava*," Zhanchi muttered, sliding his door open cautiously. From the looks of things, those Americans were going to need some help.

Chapter Three
Foreigners are not Molested

Wugong wasn't sure why he felt chilled, standing at the head of his gang and waiting for the idiots in the cab to realize they were surrounded. Admittedly, it was November and a bit chilly, but this wasn't that sort of cold. If he didn't know himself better, he'd think he was scared. But why?

It wasn't the second car, the one following his quarry into trouble. Its driver was obviously a youngster who didn't know how to handle a pursuit. He'd plenty of chances to force the cab into a blind alley and he'd ignored them all. If Wugong's men hadn't interfered by getting in the cab driver's way, the young fool would still be following behind like a little lost puppy.

Nor was it their location. The Old City was a tangled maze and they were near its center. The cab was trapped in a dead end, with his men surrounding it on either side and the stranger's car behind, blocking its escape. He had those foreign devils exactly where he wanted them. Yet he still felt like something was wrong. He just couldn't think what.

Noticing the second driver get out, he ordered, "Leave if you want to live." He kept his focus on the cab, watching for weapons or any attempt to escape. If only he'd realized the man he'd attacked aboard the *Empress* was the one he'd been sent to capture this would have been unnecessary. He'd have grabbed Conall McLeod and left that foolish woman behind.

The sound of a car door being slammed into someone's chest made Wugong turn. The other driver had gone straight for the attack before Wugong's man could open his mouth to speak. Automatically, Wugong drew on his magic, flinging a centipede at the youngster, only to have the boy break the spell with magic near twin to Wugong's own.

Shocked, Wugong took a closer look at the boy. "It's you!" he gasped.

" HE HAD THOSE FOREIGN DEVILS
RIGHT WHERE HE WANTED THEM. "

It'd been five years since he'd seen him last and Wushan had done some growing since then but he knew those intense dark eyes, broad cheekbones and that stubborn chin anywhere; they were too like their father's for him to be anyone else. He even wore his hair like father's, a short brush cut that made him look older than his seventeen years. "Younger brother?"

"Wugong?" Wushan was staring at him in turn, a look of disbelief turning to horror as he realized the implications of Wugong's current position and the sort of men he commanded. "Big brother?"

Five, even three, years ago, it would have embarrassed Wugong to admit himself a criminal, a thief and a murderer, misusing the family magic for personal gain. That was before he'd become The Foot of the Soong clan, however.

Wugong was about to order his men to remove his brother and his foreign master from the area when someone started playing a flute. It was the strangest sound, echoing soft and low through the alleyway, so diffuse its source couldn't be identified. "What the hell is that?" he demanded, looking for the player. A cloud must have covered the sun momentarily, because he felt a chill shadow cross him, sending an involuntary shudder up his spine. Other members of his gang cried out, a wave of terror following the shadow's wake.

The sound of footsteps drew Wugong's attention and he turned to see a white-haired old man walking towards them up the road. His face was partially hidden by his hands and his long brush of hair hid his face as he played a long silver flute. Whoever he was, he didn't belong in this place. Indeed, Wugong had the strangest feeling he didn't belong in this time, despite being impeccably dressed in a white silk European suit and tie.

They all stared at the stranger as he approached, until he stopped just on the other side of the cab and lowered his flute. When he raised his face, Wugong stared, for white hair aside, the man's features were those of a young man, smooth-skinned and austere, with a proud hook to the nose that suggested some foreign ancestor. It was the stranger's eyes that drew attention, though, for they were completely white. It hit Wugong suddenly, from the way the man moved and carried himself that he was quite blind.

((((

As Mudan stared at the newcomer, unsure what part he had to play in the tangled mess they'd landed in, the young man driving the other car demanded angrily in Cantonese, "What are you playing at, brother?"

"Be quiet, Wushan. I'm busy."

"I'm Zhanchi now!" the young man snapped, "And what will mother say when she finds out what you've become?"

"Zhanchi? Really? What an auspicious name. What does mother think of you taking flight?" The last was recognition that, written the right way, Zhanchi meant Spreading Wings.

"Never mind what she thinks of me. I'm fifth son! I don't matter. You're oldest! You do!"

"I matter to myself first, Wushan. What are you doing here, anyway, playing games and being some foreign devil's footrest?"

The foreign devil must be the man sitting in the back seat of the other car. Mudan could just see him, a tall thin man with features that put her in mind of the movies' portrayal of the devil: dark, dour, with a grimly elegant goatee. From his expression he was furious and she wondered if he understood a word of what the two brothers were saying.

The white haired stranger set a hand on the cab's roof and leaned close to speak to Mudan through the slightly cracked window. "You have an interesting piece of jewelry," he said in oddly accented Mandarin, ignoring the fierce argument.

"I do," she admitted in the same language.

"Take care of it and it will care for you."

Mudan wasn't entirely sure what that meant but she agreed without argument. It was important to her God and that was more than enough reason to guard it carefully.

"Then I have nothing more to say to you." The stranger tapped on the window beside the cabbie and added, "I think this would be a good time to leave, child. They are almost done and Feng Wugong is not one to remain peaceful for long."

The cabbie shook his head and it occurred to Mudan that the stranger couldn't be as blind as he seemed, given he responded to the gesture. "Why not?"

"Can't go through a brick wall, Bai She."

As Mudan realized the cabbie knew this man, Bai She said softly, "Then allow me to provide you an exit." He stood straight and that same cold darkness that had swept over everyone earlier returned. It pressed the men blocking the path to their side away, creating an opening. Their cab driver took immediate action, twisting the wheel and sending the cab flying backwards between the men and to freedom.

A minute later the other car drove after them, but when their driver asked if he should attempt to escape, Striker said, "I recognized his passenger. I'm not sure why they followed us but there's no need to run. Take us where I told you earlier." He paused, watching the scenery go past them in reverse and added, "Though you might want to turn around, first."

As their driver turned the car forward, Mudan saw the other man wave at her in an embarrassed sort of way. It relieved her mind, for there was something so like her cousin Tan at his most innocent in the young man's expression that she couldn't help being disarmed. At least for the moment.

"I just hope the engine doesn't give out," Conall said suddenly.

"She isn't accustomed to so much excitement, that's true. But I promise my lovely *Yancai* will get us there." The cabbie patted the dashboard in a way Mudan recognized only too well. Conall behaved the same way towards his favorite car.

"She does have a good engine," Conall agreed. "I can hear it. But that ride was a bit of a strain. If you'd like, I can take a look at it when we reach Sir Bruce's."

"Oh, I could never ask a patron to do such a thing, sir."

"It'd be a pleasure. What sort of engine is it?"

As Conall and their driver contented themselves with discussing matters Mudan happily ignored, she leaned back and considered their recent adventure. Absently, she traced the delicate shape of the silver bracelet she'd taken from that gangster—Feng Wugong, apparently—and wondered what it was and why it was so important.

And what Bai She—if that truly were his name—expected her to do with it.

((((

Back in the Old City, Bai She had other things on his mind than Mudan or her bracelet. She was a sensible young woman—a necessity in any Priestess of Meng Huang Shang—and not likely to act impulsively. The others, however, posed a problem, especially if they were the ones who'd captured the rest of the living metal escaped from his homeland.

Surrounded by agents of the Soong gang, including one of the gang's chiefs, he needed to find a way out of this situation with the minimum of bloodshed, his own included. Here in the human world he was far from the source of his power and not quite as immortal as usual.

Summoning the shadows attached to his spirit to act as his eyes, Bai

She searched out the leader of this group. Cripple "The Foot" and the rest of the body would be unable to stand and fight. Then, fingers lashing out in imitation of fangs, he struck, catching a wrist and almost managing to catch a nerve. He and Wugong traded blows rapidly, his fingers coming near to breaking bones and tearing skin.

"I'll kill you, blind man. You made me lose my prey for the second time!"

"So sorry to have been an inconvenience," Bai She countered, feeling the cobblestones beneath his feet shift. Old City's streets were in disrepair, complicating fighting. He was just glad its citizens had the sense to stay away. He could hear a few in the distance, watching the fight with that mix of fear and fascination that seemed to be a non-combatant's first reaction. One was even taking bets on who would win and he made a note to himself to thank the one young woman for having enough faith in him to believe he could. It was a small thing, but it made him feel better.

Something crawled up his arm, its myriad legs telling him it was a centipede of some sort. A magically summoned centipede, he realized a moment later, feeling it bite his wrist. No true insect could poison him, after all. He snatched the thing free of his arm and broke it into pieces as quickly as possible.

Shrugging off the poison, Bai She recognized his danger. His shadows could keep the other gangsters from reaching him but they couldn't block Feng Wugong's magic. One bite was manageable for a while. Two would be difficult. Three or more and it would be impossible for him to fight.

For Wugong to summon more centipedes, however, he would need to concentrate his magic. Determined not to allow his enemy that luxury, Bai She shifted his flute's shape, the living metal transforming to the whip that was his favored weapon. It snapped out and caught hold of Wugong's wrist, dragging his hand out of whatever gesture it was he was trying to make and stopping the man from summoning another centipede.

They danced around each other, Bai She spinning and twisting so as to keep the gangster off balance. He didn't need to fight for long but he had to keep Wugong from going after that girl again. The thing she guarded was a small part of a greater whole but even that small part was more power than a man like Wugong had a right to.

As they fought, Bai She heard an unfamiliar sound above him. Through his shadow sight he could see its shape: almost like a dragon, but with a body more like a horse than a serpent. Wings like a bat's carried it in a circle above the fight. He could hear the people screaming as it dove past them, the wind from its wings sending dust, pebbles and leaves flying.

The distraction gave Wugong the chance to summon several more centipedes, their bites containing enough venom to kill a human. Bai She knew one more would be sending him back to Khaitan the hard way. Hooking his fingers, he twisted them against Wugong's windpipe with bruising force and dropped him to the ground, gasping for air.

The monster was coming back for more and Bai She felt his danger before he heard it. Whatever the creature was, it was hot and growing hotter. His shadows scattered and he knew the creature was shining too bright for them to bear. Behind him he heard someone crying and realized that if he moved the monster's flames would engulf the man left behind when the crowd had scattered.

Coldly angry, Bai She lifted his face to the monster as it approached. As fast as he could, he transformed to his most basic of forms. Surrounded by the purest and coldest of waters, he flung himself into the air and bit down on his enemy's throat. Steam rose as his waters encircled the monster and it screamed and shook him free.

Tumbling to the ground, Bai She was sure he'd lost, but apparently his enemy had had enough. Shrieking curses in a strange, guttural language, the creature flew away to leave Bai She sprawled in a tangled coil, his long serpent body too weak from the poison to do anything more.

Human hands touched him and he blearily struggled to break free. But these hands were gentle and protective and he realized the folk who'd been watching the fight had come to help. Given no choice, he allowed them to drag him out of the street. Someone said something about the river and he managed to whisper, "No. A well is better."

They understood and he was soon relieved to feel the cold stone of a well head beneath his scales. Then they sent him in, allowing him to drive his way down into the darkness that was his natural home. Only when he was safely denned did Bai She relax, feeling waves of nausea and weakness from the poison working through his system. He hadn't failed his mission, but for the moment he could not continue it.

He only hoped his partner could handle things until he recovered.

((((

Chapter Four
Every Visitor Will Want a Chinese Feast

It was near sunset when they reached their destination. Sir Bruce Franer's house was one of several large, beautifully designed, older buildings along a quiet street. Surrounded by bushes, it was just possible to see a well-kept lawn around the house. The front porch had pale columns holding up a stone balustrade and the wooden door was heavily polished mahogany. In the soft light of the setting sun the building gleamed like gold.

As they parked in the driveway the other car glided in alongside it. The driver quickly opened the door for his passenger and as Conall helped Mudan out, she saw the man stare at them with a hard and suspicious expression. Then he turned to Striker. "You led us on a fine chase." His accent was high, nasal and almost stereotypically British to the point of near parody.

"If I'd expected you to meet us at the wharf I would have waited, Murtagh. You did say we'd meet here for dinner, didn't you?"

Murtagh sighed. "I did. I happened to see you getting into that cab when I was passing and thought I might as well follow. I didn't expect your driver to behave as if he were in an American gangster movie. Nor mine, for that matter."

Both the cabbie and Murtagh's driver looked at each other with identical smirks. They'd been enjoying themselves, possibly too much. She didn't show her exasperation, knowing this was not the time to draw the British man's attention. Contenting herself with a dark look that promised trouble for both drivers if they made such a mistake again, she settled herself to wait.

Once Murtagh had been mollified, Striker drew Conall forward. "You'll remember I said I knew a talented young engineer back home in Strikersport," he said by way of introduction. "This is Conall McLeod of McLeod Motors. His father worked with Tesla, you know. Conall, this is James Murtagh, one of the members of the British-Oriental Consortium."

The two men shook hands and Murtagh was about to turn to the house, ignoring Mudan. Except Conall, to Mudan's annoyance and gratification, refused to move. "We mustn't neglect the lady," Conall said. "This is Mudan Chang, Mr. Murtagh. She's here as an interpreter, among other things. Her father runs Jeen Loon Enterprises, so she's familiar with Shanghai."

That drew Murtagh's attention and he looked at her sharply. "Chang?" he repeated. "Jeen Loon Enterprises? I think I may have heard of your father, young lady. Though rumor has it that his business isn't always on the up and up."

Mudan smiled sweetly, cursing Conall's insistence on including her. "Rumor would have many things be true," she replied, thickening her accent. "I have even heard it said that one of our ancestors was the infamous pirate queen, Ching Shih, who mated with an exiled prince of dragons. But that, I think, is surely exaggeration. Certainly none of my immediate family show signs of scales or the ability to command lightning."

Before Murtagh could find an answer, the front door to the house opened and an older man strode out with wide open arms. He was a short, heavyset, fellow with greying brown hair, watery blue eyes and naïve features. Dressed in jodhpurs and a short tweed jacket with high, shiny, boots, he looked as if he'd been riding recently, for his hair and the big red silk ascot around his neck appeared rumpled.

Before anyone could open their mouths to speak, the man boomed in a stentorian voice, "My man said there were people out front just standing there but he didn't tell me it was you! Murtagh, old fellow, old chap, you didn't say you were coming over. Striker, my dear sir, I was expecting you and your companion…. oh, and a lovely young lady as well. Come in! Come in! I've no doubt you're hungry and tired and desperately in need of a good meal. My cook is putting together an authentic Chinese dinner for you and I'm sure she'll be delighted that you're here in time to eat it!"

((((

Having eaten with the Chinese workers back home, Conall thought he knew what to expect. He was wrong. This meal was larger, more elaborate and far more elegant than anything Conall had eaten from any cuisine. Plates of jellyfish, a finely sliced raw fish, conch, and abalone were followed by bowls of soup Mudan told him were made with shark's fin. Tender cuts of chicken with crispy skin were joined by dishes of garlicky vegetables. The lobster, still in its shell and covered with a sauce that made it impossible to eat neatly, was followed by steamed fish, strange black noodles, and rice mixed with chopped up vegetables. Dessert consisted of a sweet white soup, little pies filled with custard and some peach-shaped steamed breads filled with what he knew to be red-bean paste.

Fortunately, with Mudan beside him to warn him of dishes he wasn't prepared for, Conall made it through the meal without making himself sick. He excused his failure to eat as much as their host—a man with prodigious appetite—with the explanation that he was unaccustomed such rich food. Mudan keeping him from eating the raw fish, or the odd black noodles, meant he had more than enough room for the chicken, the lobster, the vegetables, and the red-bean paste dumplings. The last was a favorite back home, although they were not nearly as good as the ones Mudan made.

After dinner, they went to Sir Bruce's sitting room. By this time Conall had been introduced to Sir Bruce's other guests. First were Joseph and Georgina Forester, an older couple from Inverness. Conall guessed by their manner, austere features and clothing that they were somewhat staid and old fashioned. They were in complete contrast to the thin, short, fellow with the overly blond hair who introduced himself as David Black, a London businessman associated with a wine company.

Then there was Lois Fletcher, a dark intense young woman who'd chosen to wear trousers and a jacket and seemed determined to make her way in what was mostly a man's world. Another was Lord William Holm, a vague dark-haired fellow with an aquiline nose and a weak jaw. He was disinterested in Conall, spending most of his time discussing something called the Paper Chase Hunt Club with Sir Bruce. Lord William's companion was a quiet Japanese woman named Hikaru Fukushima. She was pretty, with pert features and dark eyes that saw more than they admitted to. And, of course, James Murtagh, who obviously found most of the topics of discussion boring beyond measure.

The two Scots, having been seated too far to speak with Conall earlier, turned to him and Mrs. Forester asked, in thickly accented English, "McLeod, is it? My brother married a McLeod from Durness. Which line are you from, then?"

Conall was embarrassed to admit, "I'm not really sure. All I know is that my family comes from St. Kilda, in the Outer Hebrides. But we've been out of touch for almost a century, now."

They seemed disappointed, turning their attention to Striker to ask about the incident aboard the *Empress*. Not daring to comment on the subject, lest he reveal too much, Conall listened to the others. Miss Fletcher appeared to be paying close attention to Mr. Black, who even Conall could see was trying to impress her for more reasons than business. Murtagh was sitting with a glass of brandy looking bored, while Lord William was speaking animatedly with Sir Bruce about their day's ride. As for Miss Fukushima and Mudan—they both sat quietly, listening attentively without speaking.

"Missed a lovely jump towards the end, old man," Lord William said, his voice loud in a momentary lull in the conversation. "Whatever happened to you this afternoon? Didn't see you at the finish line at all. Would have worried you were hurt if your man hadn't told me otherwise."

"Ran into trouble with a water snake along the way," Sir Bruce explained. "A big fellow. Had no choice but to retreat or I'm rather afraid I'd have been badly injured. As it was, it's a good thing the monster wasn't poisonous."

"Yes, I did notice you had a bruise on your neck earlier," Mr. Forester said. "Thought perhaps you'd run into an angry peasant, or maybe one of their damned man-traps."

Seeing the puzzlement on Conall's face, Murtagh explained quietly, in a dour sort of way, "They're discussing today's meeting of the Shanghai Paper Chase Hunt."

"Paper chase?"

"Yes. You see, there is a dearth of wild animals in Shanghai, so my fellow Englishmen, being unable to do without fox-hunting entirely, have had to make do with a substitute."

The statement puzzled Conall a bit, for he was almost certain he'd spotted a small dark-furred fox during their drive through what Mudan had told him was the Old City. Deciding not to argue, he asked instead, "How does it work?"

"Someone goes ahead of the hunt to set out sheets of paper—different colors have different meanings—and the Hunt rides all over the countryside, spreading chaos and confusion behind them in a grand free-for-all that achieves the desired goal of exercise, entertainment and enraging every farmer for miles around. Which, when you think about it, is not that much different from the way things are back home in England. With the notable exception of a fox-tail at the end."

Sir Bruce protested. "James, you, yourself, have been known to indulge."

"Only for the sake of business, Bruce. You know I share Oscar Wilde's opinion of the whole thing. The unspeakable in pursuit of the inedible."

"You only say that because you lost the last three hunts," Lord William countered, to Murtagh's obvious dismay.

From the way the conversation turned after that, Conall had a feeling this was part of a longstanding debate. Unable to join in and still not really understanding, he looked around for Mudan, and realized that she'd left the room.

Worried, but unwilling to draw attention, Conall hesitated only a moment. He wasn't needed here and it was too warm anyway. Ample reason for an unsocial and bookish engineer to go for a walk. Besides, he wanted to find Mudan. There were things he had to ask her, not least about what that strange, long-haired man in the silver and white robe had wanted.

⟨⟨⟨

Lacking anything better to do, Zhanchi wiped the window of Murtagh's car for what was probably the fifteenth time. His mind still raced, anxiously replaying the afternoon's chase.

Wugong was in Shanghai and it wasn't to drag his wandering brother home. He'd thought Wugong had gone to study in Peking. What had happened to bring him all the way to Shanghai? More importantly, what had happened to turn him into a criminal and to willingly turn the family magic to murder? Their family was impoverished and had long since been forced to leave their ancestral lands but they had pride of place to keep them honorable.

Whatever Wugong's reasons, Zhanchi was in no position to judge, having broken with the family himself. Disinterested in their tradition of mysticism and magic, he'd run away from home months earlier to follow in his distant uncle Feng Ru's footsteps, seeking the sky behind the controls of an airplane. Yet he'd done so out of desperate desire for flight, not to cause his parents pain.

Thinking on it, Zhanchi realized his older brother, always something of a bully, had fallen in with criminals because it was where he belonged. Zhanchi didn't like it but he wouldn't sadden his parents by sending them word of their oldest son's doings unless he had no choice. Better to let them believe Wugong still the dutiful and obedient oldest son, increasing his family's position by increasing his own.

At last Zhanchi relaxed enough to realize he'd not eaten for hours. Upset as he'd been, even the smell of excellent food hadn't attracted him. Now the last scent of the feast was gone from the air. Even so, it seemed to him that he might be able to beg something from the kitchen. This wouldn't be the first time he'd looked at a cook with big eyes and offered to help clean for scraps.

The kitchen was towards the back of the mansion; part of the building instead of a separate shed as any sensible person would have it. The path between the garage and the mansion was well cared for, so Zhanchi had no trouble reaching the back door. Even if it'd been rougher, the light from the waxing moon was enough to show him the way.

The door to the kitchen was slightly open and Zhanchi could feel warm air blow past him. No doubt the cook and her assistants had left it ajar to clear the heat from cooking. He paused, listening for people, not wanting to just walk right in. That was how one got beaten with a rice paddle.

Voices made him stop and his eyes widened as he heard a woman speaking in Hanchow's dialect. "Did you give him enough opium?"

Zhanchi stepped to the window and peeked through to see a tall woman wearing a white jacket standing in the center of the kitchen, her thick dark hair pulled back at the nape of her neck away from broad, strong features. Two men were with her, dressed in servants' clothes, simple trousers and neat grey jackets. The one was busily cleaning, while the other faced the woman with what looked to Zhanchi like a terrified expression.

"I obeyed your command and put the opium in the man's black noodles," the servant said meekly. "But he did not touch them. Nor would he take so much as one slice of *tun*."

"What? How dare he dismiss my cooking?"

"It was Striker's woman who stopped him, Mistress Zhi Lin. And no one else persuaded him to eat."

"Striker's woman? That little girl? Did she tell him why?"

"She did not speak. Just looked on him and he obeyed." The man hesitated before adding hesitantly, "I dared not cross her, Mistress. Not in front of everyone."

The 'little girl' had to be the Chinese-American woman, the one who looked so meek and demure but spoke with such certainty. Zhanchi remembered Murtagh's reaction to her earlier and wondered what, exactly, the Jeen Loon actually were. More importantly, he wondered what the cook was up to, trying to poison McLeod. Opium was bad enough, but badly prepared *tun* could paralyze and kill in minutes. Zhanchi didn't like the man's presence but why would anyone want to stop him from doing the job he'd come to do?

That question was on someone else's mind as well. A slim dark figure stepped into the kitchen from the inside door. Dressed in black trousers and shirt, with her silver bracelet glittering against her wrist, Mudan Chang no longer looked nearly so meek, nor so demure, as she had earlier. Her dark eyes had an expression that promised trouble. "My apologies for my interruption, Madam Cook. But I have questions only you can answer."

Watching the cook's hand slip over the hilt of her cleaver, Zhanchi realized that she wouldn't waste time with discussion. Not wanting to see Miss Chang's pretty face cleaved in half, he moved quickly, stepping through the back door to say, "Before you answer her, do you think you could spare some food for a hungry pilot?"

Chapter Five
Six Million Persons in China Die From Causes Other Than Natural Ones

Mudan fought to keep her expression as serene as possible, and not just to keep the chef from guessing her thoughts. If she gave her true feelings free rein, she'd start giggling foolishly right then and there, especially at the expression on her enemy's face.

Looking at the cook, Mudan was almost certain she knew who the woman had to be. Zhi Lin, the Black Orchid Assassin. No other killer was as well known for dishes that patrons would risk death for. Now Mudan was glad to have kept Conall from eating the fish. It was obviously that delicacy among connoisseurs; *tun,* a fatal dish if the chef erred at all in preparing it. If it had been the only questionable item on the menu she'd have let it slide, presuming it to be a display of wealth. The opium, hidden away in Conall's bowl of squid-ink noodles, however, had been worse than suspicious.

"Just a few bits of meat from your scraps," Zhanchi was saying. "Or a steamed bun. Or if you're feeling particularly generous, a lard cake. I'm sure you could manage a lard cake." He had the most innocent of looks on his face, the hopeful and winsome smile of a small child waiting to be given a treat.

"Young man, you do not belong in my kitchen," Zhi Lin said coldly. "Shall I send for the houseman to take you back to the garage?"

He evaded one of Zhi Lin's helpers, saying, "All I'm asking is a bit of food. My master will be here for hours yet, if I know him, and he has not even considered that his loyal pilot is dying of starvation."

Zhi Lin growled softly and Mudan saw her fingers tighten momentarily on the hilt of her cleaver. Quickly, Mudan moved in turn, sliding past Zhi Lin to catch hold of a bulb of garlic. "Why, if you have not eaten," she said smoothly, "I will gladly help you."

If Zhi Lin hadn't feared drawing attention from the rest of the house she'd have swung the cleaver immediately. Fortunately for both Mudan and Zhanchi, an assassin needed stealth if they were to do their job properly. Any obvious fight would risk revealing her true nature.

"No, my dear. Do not trouble yourself. Allow me." Zhi Lin hip-checked Mudan, forcing her off to the side as her cleaver came within inches of Mudan's hand. "Meat scraps, you say? I can provide those." From the way she moved, it was Mudan's own flesh she planned to offer.

Before Zhi Lin could get the blade closer, Mudan put her hand on the woman's and slid along with her. To the uninitiated, it would have appeared as if she were showing the cook how to use the blade. "Before my honored mother died, she taught me to hold it like this," she murmured in Zhi Lin's ear, wrapping her fingers tight. Her other hand caught hold of the woman's other wrist, forcing the cook to catch hold of the pork left over from making the stock for the shark-fin soup.

"She trained in Canton, then?" Zhi Lin kicked backwards, trying to break Mudan's knee, but Mudan twisted out of the way just in time.

"She did," Mudan agreed. "She also taught me a way to use boiled pork." Using the blade, she began slicing the meat thin, adding, "Zhanchi, stoke the fire and put the wok on." She wasn't sure the young man would catch on, but he was smarter than he looked. He dodged beneath one of Zhi Lin's assistants and caught hold of the pan, then twisted out of the way of the other, using his knee to slam the first backwards.

"Do you wish oil, Mistress Chang?"

"Not yet, silly boy," Mudan answered. "Not until the wok is hot. Get me that sauce over there. No, not that one. You don't want that. The dark brown one." The first jar was all too obviously Zhi Lin's opium.

"Hoisin," Zhi Lin said. "I see. To make up for the blandness of the boiled pork."

"Yes." Mudan spun Zhi Lin round so they were facing the vegetable basket and took an elbow in the belly as they moved. She almost lost her grip on her enemy but managed by sheer finger strength to hold on. Zhi Lin was an excellent assassin but she depended on poisons and drugs to do her work. She wasn't as strong as Mudan.

They kept moving, Zhi Lin trying to break free, her helpers trying to hurt or kill Zhanchi, all while cooking Zhanchi's dinner. With Zhi Lin between her and the wok, in a position that would set the assassin's clothing afire if she tried anything too ambitious, Mudan stir-fried the vegetables, threw the pork into the wok and added a generous dollop of hoisin sauce. She'd have included more garlic and ginger, but slicing those had proved too complicated using Zhi Lin as her puppet.

The food was just finished and Zhanchi was making pleased noises at the smell rising in the air, when the door to the kitchen opened and Conall looked in puzzledly. "Mudan? I've been looking all over for you. I know Chinese food is supposed to go right through you, but after that meal how can you possibly be hungry again?"

Mudan opened her mouth, at a loss for words, and was relieved of the need to answer by the sound of a scream somewhere towards the front of the house. "OH MY GOD HE'S DEAD!"

⦗⦗⦗

The scream would have made Conall return to Sir Bruce's sitting room, but he was more concerned about Mudan, whose expression combined annoyance, exasperation, fear and a desperate desire to laugh. He knew Mudan well and he could tell she was afraid. That woman whose wrists Mudan held so tightly was surely the cook and there was only one reason Mudan would be treating anyone that way.

Whatever the circumstances, Conall would have to wait for answers. "We should find out what's going on," he began, only to find himself under attack from one of the kitchen staff, the man wielding a large and very sharp looking knife.

Mudan spun the cook around and flung her against a wall as hard as she could, then slammed her foot into the other man's wrist. At the same time Zhanchi, or whatever his name was, flung the contents of the wok at the face of the other helper. "What a waste," he muttered in Chinese. "I really was looking forward to that."

"I'll make something for you later," Mudan snapped. "Zhi Lin's getting away!" She was too busy keeping the man attacking Conall at bay to go

" MUDAN SPUN THE COOK AROUND AND FLUNG
HER AGAINST THE WALL — "

after the cook. The woman was gone before either could react, however, and Mudan sighed. "Never mind."

"Oh, wait, I'm in luck," Zansi said. "There's a bit left in the pot." He grabbed a pair of chopsticks from the nearby container and stuffed his mouth with meat, even as he kicked his opponent in the kneecap, knocking him down.

Conall, not wanting to be left out, caught hold of Mudan's 'partner' in the fight and swung him around, landing an uppercut on the man's jaw that would have made his friend George proud. It wasn't enough to knock the fellow out but Mudan finished him off with a sharp kick to the side that sent him staggering into a barrel in the corner. Zansui caught hold of his enemy's nose with his chopsticks and used them to keep the man still long enough to punch him in the belly, knocking him into the barrel right after the first. To Conall's relief, the young driver dropped the chopsticks in after and got new, clean, ones from the container.

"This," Zansei said in English for McLeod's benefit, "is very good. *Tai haole.*"

"Not enough garlic or scallions," Mudan complained, tasting the sauce. "Not my best work at all."

Conall grinned, despite the tension of the moment. "You were distracted. And shouldn't we be finding out what's going on up front? You too, Zonesa, your boss might be the one they're talking about."

"Zhanchi."

"Eh?"

"My name. It's not Zonesa, you blithering Western imbecile. It's Zhanchi." He spoke in English, as if to a small child.

"Oh." Conall replayed the name in his head. "Zaanchi?"

"Damnit! Zhanchi."

Mudan caught both their ears with her fingers. "This is not the time," she snapped. "Come."

They followed Mudan with expressions Conall suspected were identically bemused and embarrassed. She was right to be annoyed, given the circumstances. Even so, as they walked, Conall tried again. "Zhanchi?"

"Better. Your Chinese is excruciating. Stick to English."

"If not practice, how learn?" Conall asked reasonably in Mandarin.

"Will the two of you both shut up?"

They went silent just in time as they entered the sitting room to find Miss Fletcher and Mrs. Forester holding onto each other; Miss Fukushima sitting apart looking distantly concerned; Forester, Black, Murtagh and

Striker all staring down in consternation while Lord William bent over Sir Bruce. Their host lay on his back, eyes wide and staring. "He's still breathing," Lord William said grimly. "We should get him to the hospital."

Mudan stepped forward, "There may not be time," she said. "I believe it to be *tun* poisoning."

That made Miss Fukushima sit up straight. "*Tun*. You mean *fugu?*" At Mudan's agreement, she turned to look at Lord William. "Don't bother with a doctor. There isn't an antidote. All we can do is make him vomit and hope he survives."

Conall joined Lord William in dragging the older man to a better position, remembering stories he'd heard about a Japanese dish considered so precious it was worth risking death to eat. At the same time, Mudan left the room, coming back a few minutes later with a glass. "Syrup of ipecac," she said calmly. "Help me give it to him, Conall."

It took the whole glass, but suddenly Sir Bruce was completely and comprehensibly sick all over his fine carpet. After several minutes, during which several of his servants came in, ran out, and came in again with terrified expressions and mops and pails, he was finally emptied of every ounce of dinner and more besides. The smell was beyond horrible and all Conall could do was hope he didn't add to it himself.

At last, when it seemed there was nothing more for Sir Bruce to vomit, they carried him to the couch, where he lay quiet, breathing heavily, sweat beading on his clammy forehead. It was Striker who demanded, "Whose idea was it to serve something like *fugu*? Where is the cook?"

One of Sir Bruce's servants stammered, "No knowee, meester. Cook gone runee off."

"As for the *fugu*," Murtagh said grimly, "Sir Bruce said something yesterday to me about acquiring a Japanese delicacy. It was just like him to include it without warning us first. Did anyone else eat it?"

Forester turned pale and sat down. "I did."

"You shouldn't worry too much, Mr. Forester," Miss Fukushima said gently. "You are much thinner than Sir Bruce. If you had consumed a dangerous dose of *fugu* poison we would already know."

Sir Bruce started coughing and struggled to sit up. "What's all this about, then. What is that horrible stench and why does my throat hurt?"

While his friends rushed to Sir Bruce's side, hurriedly explaining and making much over him, Conall glanced thoughtfully at Mudan. It seemed to him, based on what he'd heard about *fugu*, that the knight had recovered with suspicious speed.

The question was, had he been poisoned at all or had it been a trick? And if he had, how had he recovered so quickly?

ᴄᴄᴄ

Zhi Lin ran, ripping her cook's coat off as she made her way through the darkened streets. The deep blue silk blouse she wore beneath was less noticeable in the shadows and right now all she wanted was to get as far from Shanghai as possible. Someone had died and though, for once, she was not the killer, she doubted the authorities would see the irony. Wanted in most of China now, her neck would be on the chopping block within hours if they captured her.

At last, having kept moving for over an hour, she went to the safe house in Chapei she shared with her two assistants. The old temple was among those slated for demolition, having been declared unsafe for habitation, but its interior was still solid and sound enough for a temporary hideout. She'd wait there for her men to show up, then plan their escape.

They'd have to return to *Chinglung* Mountain. Lord Zhao wouldn't be pleased with her, but her master seldom was, even when she'd done well. It would have been worse if he'd sent her on this mission, instead of it being a hired job. Failing Zhao was seldom a healthy thing, even for his eldest daughter. Since it was just the Soong gang, however, she knew Lord Zhao would be irritated, not furious. Besides, she had information for him. An engine of near limitless power would be invaluable to his cause, even if only as a bargaining chip. It cost a great deal of money to command a small army and keep it secret.

An hour passed before Zhi Lin heard someone out in the street. She hid, listening for the tapped codes that would identify her apprentices. To her surprise, a small, slight, man entered the temple instead. She didn't know him, but the sheer number of knives he wore in his vest warned her he wasn't a wandering tramp looking for shelter.

"Wise of you to hide after nearly killing Sir Bruce," the man said in her native Hanchow. He hoisted his skinny frame onto a broken block of stone and grinned at her. "I doubt the Soong gang will be pleased to hear about it, either, given he's central to their plan."

Zhi Lin considered blowing one of her poisons in the stranger's face but something about his watchful gaze stopped her. Somehow she knew a false move would end with a knife embedded in her hand, if not her throat. Seduction was obviously impossible. Some men could be broken, others trained, but not this one. He saw too clearly, with cynical eyes that mocked both himself and the world around him. "I don't know what you're talking about," she answered with rare honesty. "I wasn't hired to kill anyone, especially not that bumbling fool."

"Sir Bruce just barely survived the pufferfish you fed him and his guests this evening. Interestingly, he was the only one to become ill. Apparently your cooking skills leave more to be desired than I'd been given to understand."

Insulted, because the thing she prided herself on most was her skill as both an assassin and a chef, Zhi Lin snapped, "If he was poisoned it was not by me. I can kill a single man out of twenty; all eating from the same platter and drinking from the same jar."

The stranger's skeptical little smile made Zhi Lin yearn to slap him. "So I'd heard. But still, he nearly died."

"I know nothing about that."

"Nothing?" The new voice came from above them and when Zhi Lin looked up she found herself face to face with horror. The creature perched atop the shattered roof was almost as big as a house, with scales that covered its long, almost lizard, almost horse-like shape. Great wings like a bat's spread behind it, blotting out the faint light from the waning moon. Its hot breath smelled of sulfur and melted rock and its voice shook the earth. "You were the cook."

Zhi Lin shrieked and would have run if the monster hadn't slithered down to block her path. Before she could move, it raised a claw, showing her what it held. A head, body just barely attached, and one she recognized; Fou, her second assistant, his dead eyes wide and empty and his mouth filled with blood. The monster drew the corpse close and licked the blood from the body's throat. "You had a job, assassin. Not only did you fail, but you put my tool at risk. I have use for Sir Bruce and I will not have him interfered with."

"I didn't poison him. And my pufferfish was safe to eat," Zhi Lin told the creature, all too aware she had no escape. A thought occurred to her, based on having cooked for Sir Bruce several weeks now. The man was a glutton. "Unless he ate the whole platter."

"You know, now that you say that," the small stranger said thoughtfully, "I seem to remember most of the guests abstained. He said something about not letting something so delicious go to waste." The interruption caused a small flare of red heat in the monster's nostrils as it turned its head to look at the speaker as he continued, "And I think some fire medicine might be in order right now."

Understanding immediately, Zhi Lin made a move towards the window and, as the creature opened its mouth to attack, she threw her bag of gunpowder straight down its throat. The resulting explosion sent the beast rocking backwards and she leapt outside, running as fast as she could.

In the minutes that followed she kept hearing a sound like cloth flapping on the wind. Then it went silent and she slowly relaxed. She'd gotten away. All she needed to do now was find a new place to hide before making her escape. It was too bad about her apprentices, but sacrifices had to be made.

She was almost to the edge of Chapei's ruins when a sound behind her made her turn. She looked up to see the big black form gliding her way, limned by the light of the waxing moon. She didn't even have a chance to scream before it opened its mouth to loose a stream of raging fire.

Chapter Six
Paper Hunting
is a Popular Sport

The party broke up soon after the excitement over Sir Bruce's illness. Mudan, having made sure Conall's room was safely next to her own, slept restlessly. The bumps and bruises she'd taken over the last two days were making themselves known and she considered herself lucky that she hadn't sprained a knee dealing with that one gangster. What was it his brother had called him? Wugong.

If Mr. Murtagh had stayed the night Mudan would have questioned the young man. She was fairly sure Zhanchi wasn't on his brother's side, but that didn't make him an ally. Not even the fact that he'd helped her fight Zhi Lin could prove that much.

Then there was the question of what Wugong was up to. Was it murder or simply abduction and either way, why? The engine Conall had been hired to examine was likely at the heart of the matter but until he examined it, there was little to be done on that count. All she could do was try to keep him safe.

Finally there was the question of the bracelet her God demanded she take from Wugong. Mudan looked at it thoughtfully, tracing the delicate shape, and wondered how it'd been made. As her father's daughter, Mudan had learned a great deal about art. She'd watched jade be carved, metals be shaped and jewels be polished and she'd never seen anything like the bracelet.

For one thing, it'd been wrapped tight around Wugong's wrist when she'd caught hold of it. It had no latch, nor join, to open. Yet it'd slid free of the criminal's arm and onto hers as if made of water or quicksilver. It was magic, that much was obvious, but so far she'd seen and felt nothing to suggest its nature.

No, that wasn't quite right. At first the bracelet had seemed cold, a solid piece of metal that glittered prettily on her arm. But it was beginning to grow warmer and had been ever since they'd met that pale-haired man back in the Old City. 'Take care of it and it will take care of you,' he'd said, and she'd agreed without hesitation.

She eyed the design: a slim Chinese dragon with delicate whiskers and the finest of manes. Its eyes glittered at her and as she gazed into them, one seemed to wink. On the assumption that any magical item might have a will and mind of its own, she told it, "I have promised my protection. I keep my promises, but you must not cause trouble. I have work to do and I will not have it interrupted."

Some sense came to her of a small child trying desperately to show how innocent it was. Deciding that was the closest she'd get to a promise and being unsure what the thing could do anyway, she said reassuringly, "You are small and I think you are not strong yet. Wait and bide. Your time will come."

Then, having satisfied herself that there was nothing more she could do about the troubles that faced them, Mudan turned out her light and went to sleep.

《《《

"I still don't believe this."

Conall, who'd been staring out the window as their hired driver took them through Shanghai, looked at Striker. His employer had been complaining from the moment they'd risen until now over Sir Bruce's plans. Last night Striker had agreed to join the knight on one of those hunts they'd been talking about. After Sir Bruce became ill he'd been sure the plan was scotched, but was disabused of that notion at breakfast.

"I just hope I can persuade him I can't ride," Conall replied. He'd never been on a horse in his life and had no wish to start now.

"I would prefer it if you did not ride, either," Mudan added. "For that matter, I would prefer not to be so out in the open. There is no point in making it easy for someone to harm you. Not when I am not permitted to join you." She wasn't dressed for riding, anyway, having chosen a loose grey tweed skirt and jacket over an ivory silk blouse.

Striker considered the question and called forward to the driver. "Shen, wasn't it?" he said. "Do you know a place where these two could go while I'm occupied? Preferably enclosed, with easy exits."

"The answer is before you," Shen answered. "Seek and you shall find." He gestured towards an attractive old building, one that resembled some of the houses in the residential district of Strikersport's Chinatown. "Jing'an Temple and cemetery. The famed bubbling well that gives this road its name is here, as well as many small shrines, some half-forgotten in favor of the Buddha's worship. If you wish, I will bring your young companions back to view the place."

Striker raised an eyebrow at Mudan to make sure she agreed. At her slight nod, he told Shen, "That sounds like a great idea. You three do that and I'll do my best to play along with Sir Bruce." Ruefully, he added, "As well as my best not to fall off. You're not the only one unaccustomed to riding, McLeod."

A few minutes later the cab came to a halt alongside several dozen other large and beautifully kept vehicles, one of which Conall recognized as belonging to Murtagh. And, no surprise, Zhanchi was leaning against it, watching the excitement as several dozen men dressed in riding clothes were trying to get their horses in line and calmed down.

Shen climbed out and assisted Mudan from the cab. "I will wait here until you're ready to tour the temple."

They went on to find Sir Bruce arguing with Lord William towards the center of the hunt club's preparations. "My dear old chap, I'm quite well and more than ready for a ride. No need to worry for me. Took the air for a bit last night to clear my head and even managed to find myself a snack on the way. It wasn't all I wanted, but it was enough."

Lord William eyed Sir Bruce critically. "I don't know, old boy. You still sounded a bit off this morning."

"Broke a tooth on that snack, that's all. Just fine now, I promise." Sir Bruce turned to look at Striker, Conall and Mudan. "Ah, yes, my dear guests. I've two lovely horses for you."

"You only need one," Conall reminded the knight for what he was sure was the tenth time, "I can't ride."

"Nonsense, lad. Come along and give this fellow a try."

To Conall's dismay, Sir Bruce chivied him over to a plump brown pony that whickered at him peaceably. If he was to ride this would probably be the best animal for his very first try. Before he reached it, something small and silver flew past him. He blinked, seeing what looked like a miniature Chinese dragon clinging to the horse's mane beside its ear, as if to whisper in it.

Oblivious to the creature sitting atop the horse's head, Sir Bruce started to hand Conall the reins. Except the horse suddenly and almost apologetically tipped Sir Bruce over onto his belly by pulling backwards at just the right moment. Everyone went to the knight's aid and by the time he was on his feet again the horse had wandered off in a fit of stubbornness neither threat nor bribe could overcome.

Conall looked around for the little dragonet and spotted a flash of silver against Mudan's skirt. Seeing her calm, composed expression, he guessed he shouldn't let anyone realize what he'd noticed. At a guess the bracelet was magic. He'd have to ask her about it later, when no one was around to hear.

Realizing Sir Bruce was sulking over his spill, and his failure to get Conall a proper mount, he told the Englishman, "I really don't think I should be riding. You need my skull in one piece and I'm sure I'd break something if I tried. Especially if jumping like that is involved." He gestured towards one of the other riders, a skinny slight fellow who seemed to have been born in the saddle. He wasn't even bothering with his reins as he guided his mount over ditches and small hillocks. The sight appeared to amuse Mudan to no end for some reason. She was smiling in an oddly indulgent way.

Sir Bruce sighed "Well, that was the only horse I could find gentle enough for a new rider," he admitted. "If he's not cooperating, there's no choice. Striker, I'll introduce you to your mount. It's the biggest one I could find for you, don't worry."

Once the two men had left to join the rest of the hunt, Conall and Mudan returned to the car. "What was it about that man? The one you were watching," Conall asked. "Did you know him?"

"I have met him before, when I was much smaller. I liked him very much, but I was too young then and am not interested now." That didn't explain her amusement, Conall pointed out, and she added, "He is sometimes called the Black Jade Fox. Appropriate to the occasion, is it not?"

Conall had to admit it was. And to wonder, thoughtfully, if that meant this man was some sort of shape changer. If so, it would explain the animal he'd been sure he'd seen following them around yesterday. The only question left being, why?

《《《

Zhanchi watched the hunters disdainfully. One would have thought Sir Bruce would have decided to do without this foolishness after being so sick the night before. Even now Murtagh was complaining to anyone who'd listen that it was nonsense to indulge in another Paper Hunt already. Of course, Murtagh wanted to get to the new engine, one of the few instances when Zhanchi agreed with him.

Unfortunately, only the Americans shared his and Murtagh's distaste for the whole thing. Striker, forced to ride a pony several times too small for his long legs, was sitting uncomfortably off to the side and clearly planning on doing the very least he could reasonably do for the duration of what McLeod had called a faux-hunt.

Zhanchi grinned to himself. He might not be a native speaker of English but he recognized the pun. It'd made Mudan groan softly to herself. Of course, what good was a pun if it didn't make those around you wince?

Those two weren't riding, McLeod because he couldn't and Mudan because she wasn't permitted. Like the other ladies, she was limited to standing on the sidelines and watching. Her serene gaze appeared to be on the men preparing to ride out into the field, but Zhanchi was somehow certain her attention was really on McLeod. He wondered what Striker would think of his woman paying so much heed to the younger man.

Mudan wasn't watching McLeod now. Her eyes were on the young man assisting the hunt master and Zhanchi followed her gaze curiously. Aside from his obvious skill with a horse, there didn't appear to be anything remarkable about him. Chinese, but dressed in a modern, western style, with a flat cap and longish, fly-away hair, he looked like a street tough. Yet Mudan eyed him thoughtfully and Zhanchi heard her say softly to McLeod, "It is he who lays the trail, I see. A fox hunt indeed."

The horn sounded and the riders set off, racing over the broad fields. Zhanchi could see Murtagh near the lead, proving that despite his hatred of the hunt, he was too competitive to do anything but his best. Striker was somewhere towards the middle, struggling to stay mounted. As for Sir

Bruce, as usual, he'd gone off in the wrong direction. Already he was far out of sight and no one could tell him so; even if he'd listen.

As the hunt faded off in the distance, Zhanchi rubbed his hands together against the November chill, glad the day was at least sunny. It'd be sheer hell if it started raining, or worse, snowing, during the chase. At least the spectators could demand to be driven back to the clubhouse. He was expected to wait for the race to be over.

Worse, it would be a while before the silly fools were done, meaning all Zhanchi could do was sit and wait. Noticing McLeod and Mudan climbing back into their cab and the driver preparing to take them elsewhere, curiosity got the better of him. He went over and tapped on the window on McLeod's side.

"Is problem?" McLeod was still attempting to speak Chinese and while his accent was as atrocious as ever, he was comprehensible. From behind him, Mudan corrected his pronunciation and he adjusted it. Still not right, but better than most Westerners, Zhanchi reflected. "You have message?"

To make things easier, Zhanchi replied in English. "No. But Mr. Murtagh would be happier if you didn't go wandering all over Shanghai right now. Sir Bruce may be too flighty to stay focused on business, but not he."

It was the driver who answered, "I'm taking them to *Jing'an* temple, child. Not far away at all." He was an arrogant looking fellow, with a high forehead, hair too long to be fashionable and a sardonic smile that suggested he considered himself superior to all around him. Not, Zhanchi thought, the sort of man one would expect to find driving a taxicab.

Zhanchi might have quibbled over someone barely five, maybe ten, years his senior calling him 'child'. Instead he said, "In that case, let me come with you." It wasn't interest in McLeod's company and Mudan was too cold a fish for his tastes, but waiting for the chase to be over would be a long and boring ordeal, there being no one among the servants and drivers to talk to.

Mudan sighed. "It is becoming a habit," she said, tone combining exasperation and amusement, "this following us around. I am not entirely sure I approve."

"Your master may well be displeased, should he return to his car and not find you there," the driver told him reprovingly. "Whereas my employer has asked me to guide these two."

With a shrug, Zhanchi told the man, "Murtagh needs me to pilot his plane. As for why I followed... those two seem to run into trouble on a regular basis."

"He has point," McLeod noted, still trying to speak Chinese.

"Quiet, you. Don't help him." Mudan's tone had an indulgent note that confirmed Zhanchi's suspicion about the two of them. Striker surely wasn't going to appreciate this situation. Not that Zhanchi intended to tell anyone. "Fine. I give up. Shen, let him come with us. We will draw attention to ourselves if we continue discussing the matter here."

With a grin, Zhanchi climbed in beside Shen and looked at the two in back. "So why *Jing'an* Temple? There are plenty of things to see in Shanghai. Besides, *Lunghua* is much prettier—and it has a pagoda as well."

Shen chuckled. "I too, prefer *Lunghua* temple," he admitted. "But *Jing'an* is closer. We only have a few hours and there'd hardly be any time at all to sightsee if I took you children there."

That was true, though Zhanchi couldn't help complaining, "Children? You're barely a year or so older than I am."

"I am young, but not that young, child," Shen said serenely.

Before Zhanchi could demand particulars, McLeod changed the subject, "Did you say you were Murtagh's pilot?"

"I work for the CNAC," Zhanchi corrected. "But they allowed Murtagh to hire my services privately. They want to know about that engine as much as everyone else. Not that I've been much use. We haven't been allowed near the thing."

"Inventors do like to keep their secrets," McLeod agreed, and if there was the same doubt in his voice that Zhanchi felt, neither man admitted it.

By this time Shen had driven the short distance back up the road and parked his cab to the side, allowing his passengers a moment to gaze at their destination. "It's an attractive place," McLeod said, eyeing the cemetery, "Very peaceful. Puts me in mind of the one back home."

"There is a reason for that, Conall," Mudan told him and the American engineer agreed equably, adding, "I like the look of the temple, too."

Zhanchi eyed the place critically as they walked towards it. "It isn't so bad," he admitted. "But I still prefer *Lunghua* temple. I go there every time I fly."

Shen eyed him curiously. "Oh, really? Then are you the one who lights all the joss sticks at every shrine?"

Zhanchi blushed. "I don't know how you know that," he muttered. "But I do light them, yes."

The driver opened his mouth to say more, but the sight of dozens of men and women crowding into the courtyard of the temple stopped him. Slowly, the man said, "It seems we are not alone in choosing today to visit the Gods."

Chapter Seven
There Has Been Friction Between the Japanese & the Chinese

Raud, the Black Dragon of Sunderland and Scourge of the Downs, moved with amazing delicacy and grace, worming his way past the great doors of the former cotton mill to glare with hot and furious eyes on the boss of the Soong gang. He was a big strong beast, with gleaming black scales and eyes the color of a stormy sky. Though spawned in England, he'd gnawed at Shanghai's roots ever since the British had forced the *Dàoguāng* Emperor to cede the city to their control.

The dragon was now deeply embedded in the city's underworld, a distrusted but occasionally valuable ally to those who knew of him. The Soong gang—long allied with magical beings—had often come into contact with him. Usually enemies, this was a rare time their interests made an alliance possible. Still, no one liked, nor trusted, Raud. He was too quick to anger and too willing to kill and eat the cause of his rage.

Wugong stood as calm and still as he could while his boss, Soong Kou, faced their… partner? ally? associate? colleague? No doubt Raud thought himself something more. Whatever else he was, the dragon was very like his human counterparts. The belief in British superiority over all things Chinese was ingrained in every fiber of his being. His assumption of authority meant he considered the gang's recent failures to be a direct insult to his command.

Right now, Boss Soong was doing his best not to show his own fury. Zhi Lin wasn't a member of the gang but she was a useful and skilled tool. According to Chen Tang, who'd rescued her from the dragon at the last moment, Raud's attack had left her so badly burned that the doctor wasn't sure she'd survive. That Raud had killed both her apprentices, skilled poisoners in their own right, only made things worse. Wugong wasn't sure how that sneaky little bastard Chen had saved her. It must have been embarrassing, for Raud admitted nothing. He certainly wasn't discussing his broken fang, nor the fresh tear in his left wing flap.

Still, one didn't make one's opinions too obvious in the face of a being that could set the entire room alight with one irritated snort. Soong spoke as calmly as he could, telling Raud, "There was an unexpected complication. The girl Striker brought with him is more than she appears to be."

"Mudan Chang?" A little snort filled the air with a cloud of sulfurous smoke and set everyone coughing. Raud ignored their reaction. "She's just a little Chinese madam who thinks too well of herself." He waved one black wing, sending the smoke wafting through the warehouse.

Wugong reflected that that woman's actually being Chinese would take the sting from losing to her. But it was obvious from her way of speaking, her way of moving, that she was nothing of the sort. Everything about her spoke of an American woman pretending to be what she was not. Oh, her current disguise was a good one, Wugong had almost not recognized her in the car yesterday, but he was certain she was as American as Marlene Dietrich.

"We don't know who she works for, but it's obvious she's an agent. American, perhaps, since Striker brought her in." Soong shrugged. "What matters is that she's interfering with our efforts to capture McLeod. And until we do capture him, we continue to run the risk that he will realize our engine is not what it appears to be."

Wugong glanced involuntarily at the engine's most important component. The glass jar, half-filled with a pint of what appeared to be quicksilver, sat on a nearby table, an electronic box sealing its lid. It was being carefully monitored by the engineering students Soong had blackmailed into working for him and seemed inert. At least it did until Wugong looked at it. An eye formed amid the silver and glared back hatefully before dissipating, forced back down by a current of electricity.

Again Wugong cursed losing his bracelet. Without it, the only way they could control the quicksilver were the electrical impulses being pumped into the jar. He kept himself turned so his left arm was hidden from the jar's line of sight. The engineers were certain the stuff had no mind, but he couldn't help fearing it would realize the part he'd held was gone.

Soong was still soothing Raud's annoyance. "We have a new plan to capture McLeod," he said.

"You have the perfect chance right now. The fellow is wandering around waiting for the Hunt to finish."

"I have a man watching him," Soong said. "He is to signal if there is an opportunity to take McLeod during the Hunt. But if no such chance comes then we have another way. It will require Sir Bruce to take his guests to the Eastern Star nightclub to see the lovely Manuela."

Raud considered the plan. "And what will happen there?"

"I have men working at the Eastern Star," Soong answered, not telling the dragon he was the nightclub's owner. "They will lure McLeod from his protector and capture him. No one else will interfere; those who attend such places aren't interested in another's troubles."

After a moment, Raud agreed. He was about to say more when one of Soong's guards hurried in. "Sir," he gasped, "Zhi Lin is here with a group of Japanese. They say they're here to buy the engine but I think they're soldiers!"

⟨⟨⟨

Zhi Lin sat in a wheelchair pushed by one of her captors, pretending to be nearly unconscious. Her face and arms were wrapped in far more bandages than necessary. She'd insisted on them, knowing that looking helpless was the only way Soong would believe she hadn't betrayed the gang to the Japanese. Which, of course, she had.

Lieutenant Kurumata Katashi walked beside her. Although dressed in civilian clothes and trying to appear like a Japanese businessman, his real occupation was obvious. He was too strict, too self-disciplined and too humorless to succeed at his disguise. Long limbed, broad-shouldered, and hard-featured, he was the perfect soldier.

He and his men looked around with disapproval. The abandoned factory wasn't much of a place, Zhi Lin admitted. Just an old building among many on the northwest side of Shanghai. Once it'd been part of a cotton mill beside one of Soochow Creek's many bends, before the owners had gone bankrupt. Unable to find buyers for their aging equipment and buildings, they'd left it all to rot. From the outside it looked like a light breeze would knock it over.

The gangster who'd run inside when they'd arrived returned, looking scared. "Master Soong will see you in his office," he said. "This way."

The inside of the warehouse was a maze of shelves filled with junk and looked just as unimpressive as the outside. Tell the truth, Zhi Lin didn't know if this was where the gang was hiding their plane engine. It didn't seem like there'd be space with all these shelves. Besides, wouldn't something closer to the airfield have been better? Still, that didn't matter to her right now. Her only purpose was to keep her head attached to her

"MASTER SOONG
WILL SEE YOU IN HIS OFFICE,"

shoulders. Lord Zhao was the only one she'd grant the right to kill her.

The gangster led them through one hall, then another, then up a flight of stairs, until they were in what had once been the foreman's office high above the shop floor. There being no ramp, the man pushing Zhi Lin's wheelchair had had to pick her up and carry her. Most of the men remained below and she knew they were already searching the warehouse for the engine.

The office itself was a grimy little room with broken out windows. Once it'd been the foreman's office, overlooking the factory floor. Now all one could see below were shelves filled with boxes and bags. Weapons? Gold? Opium? Zhi Lin neither knew, nor cared. All she knew was the place stank of dust, old oil, rust and something vaguely familiar and strangely unnerving. It was too faint to identify, though, and she didn't dare ask.

Soong Kou was sitting behind the only desk, with his grim-faced watchdog, Wugong, behind him. Once everyone had been introduced, Soong said, "I understand you believe we have an engine to sell... ah... Mr. Kurumata?"

"I know you have an engine you're selling to the British-Oriental Consortium," Kurumata corrected. "My agent has kept me apprised of all the details, up to and including your recent attempts to kidnap the American hired to examine your engine."

"Kidnapping? What a base accusation! Why would we do a thing like that?" Soong leaned back in his chair and looked satisfied with himself. "We have every confidence that this American, McLeod, will have no issues with the design, nor its performance. And why, Mr. Kurumata, should it matter to you? If you're interested in joining the Consortium it's Sir Bruce you should be talking to, not me."

Kurumata looked on Soong with disdain. "Sir Bruce is a fool."

"Well, you won't get an argument from me on that count," Soong agreed amiably. "He does appear to be a very typical British lord. All bluster and hot air."

"Besides, the engine could cause my country a great deal of trouble, should it be used to build a viable air force here in China. I will not allow that. Sell me the engine and I will not have to confiscate it."

Zhi Lin snorted under her breath, "Steal, you mean," she couldn't help pointing out.

"Manchuria already belongs to Japan. Soon, China will fall to us as well," Kurumata snapped without bothering to look at her. "It is not theft to take what will be ours anyway."

Fury suffused Zhi Lin and she was glad most of her face was covered, especially when Soong said in a mollifying fashion, "Mr. Kurumata, I have no wish to fight. I will give you what you have come for."

Unable to help herself, Zhi Lin muttered, "Traitor." It was one thing for Chinese to fight and murder Chinese in the eternal dance for power. Quite another to hand over that power to an outsider. That she was cooperating with Kurumata for the sake of her own skin was something she refused to admit to herself. She'd certainly never admit it to Lord Zhao.

"I knew you would see things my way," Kurumata said, so smugly that Zhi Lin would have killed him then and there if she had the means. Then that familiar smell wafted up from the darkness below them again. With a surge of real terror, she realized the trap they'd walked right into.

That monster, the one that had eaten her men and nearly killed her. It was here.

((((

Fukushima Hikaru watched the old cotton mill from her hiding place behind a nearby work-shed. The gang's reaction to Lieutenant Kuramata's invasion had been just what she'd expected. As soon as he'd entered the building several dozen of the Soong gang's men slipped out hurriedly; rats deserting a sinking ship. They'd carried bags of money, but nothing big enough to be an airplane engine. The largest thing she saw was a glass jar filled with some silvery substance and capped with an odd boxy object. Whatever it was, it couldn't have anything to do with an engine.

Had Soong caved to Kurumata's demands? Fukushima doubted it. She wondered if she ought to follow one of the men but that was risky. Choose wrong and she'd never find where the engine was. No, the best one to follow would be a leader. Soong preferably but Wugong if necessary. That last would be tricky; the stories said Wugong was more than he seemed, and while she wasn't sure what that meant, she did know that those who crossed him seemed to end up dead of some virulent poison, their bodies covered in insect bites.

It wasn't long after Kurumata entered that the flames started. A few flickers at first but brightening quickly. She hesitated, unsure what to do. The mission depended on her finding the engine, but so far she'd seen no sign of either Soong or Wugong.

Sighing, she slipped inside the building, aware of her danger but needing to find her targets. Rather than search through the twisted passages created by all the shelves, she simply climbed up the closest one, keeping close watch on the fire at the other end of the building.

There were screams and curses coming from the direction of the flames and she heard someone running wildly in the shadowy darkness. Then she spotted the monster crawling over one of the distant shelves and she had to fight back a startled cry. It hadn't noticed her, or at least she prayed it hadn't, and she took the chance to slip down one shelf so she was out of sight. Fortunately she'd chosen to dress for the occasion, in dark grey work-clothes and gloves. She even had a hood to cover her face should that become necessary. Not that she gave much for her chances if that monster could smell her out.

Somewhere above, Kurumata shouted from a blocky structure attached to the ceiling. "What's going on down there?" he roared furiously in Japanese. "Someone put out that fire!"

No one answered; though whether they were too scared, too injured or too dead wasn't clear. What did reply was more than enough to send chills down any sane person's spine. "Why put out the flames," the voice purred. "I like the flames. They suit me. They become me." Strangely, Fukushima heard the words in both English and Japanese, as if the monster were speaking a tongue her mind could only comprehend through the languages she knew. "And I become them."

A scream followed the voice's boast and a moment later Fukushima saw the monster rise up from between the shelves again, a human body struggling in its jaws. Fire blazed around the figure, the smell of charred meat filling the air as the monster bit down and swallowed. She winced for the victim and knew she had no choice but to escape. She'd heard rumors of this horror, a European dragon who'd burrowed its way into Shanghai's underworld, but she'd thought it mere superstition. Yet there it was and if it found her, her mission would end the worst possible way.

Gunfire drew the monster's attention back the way it'd come and it laughed, sliding back towards its attackers. Screams and more flames followed and Fukushima spotted Kurumata running onto the walkway, watching his command burn expressionlessly. He raised his pistol, about to fire, and Fukushima had to make a quick decision. He was still valuable to her mission. No matter how little she liked him she couldn't leave him to die. Not yet.

Twisting out from between the shelves, Fukushima climbed up a nearby ladder and leapt for the walkway, catching hold of Kurumata just barely in time. The monster reared his head up over the shelves and breathed a stream of fire towards the Lieutenant as she dragged him out of the way. "Let go of me!" he screamed, trying to break free.

Fukushima twisted him around by the wrist. "Your men are dead! You will be too and unable to avenge them if you remain!" she snapped. "Run!"

He stared at her, confused, but some survival instinct made him obey. They both ran for the end of the walkway, crashing through the window facing Soochow Creek. Luck was with them. They flew through the air, splashed into the water and were carried along with the current before the monster could follow.

As the creature's bellows filled the air like a siren, Fukushima dove deep and prayed something with such a strong affinity for fire would not dare the waves.

Chapter Eight
Bubbling Well Temple is Well Worth Seeing

The crowd in *Jing'an* temple's courtyard puzzled Zhanchi. It was a weekend and a beautiful day but even those things didn't ordinarily draw so many. Watching the men, women and children, he realized they weren't visiting the temple, but the well in front.

"What is happening?" Mudan asked curiously as they paused at the edge of the crowd. She asked in Chinese and one of the old women nearest them turned and looked at her. Disapproval faded from the withered features as Mudan bowed to the woman, offering the proper respect a girl her age owed her elders. "Apologies, grandmother. I was speaking to my friends and did not mean to interrupt you."

The old woman considered her a moment and smiled almost toothlessly. "You are not from Shanghai."

"This insignificant daughter of the Chang was born in America, grandmother, in a place called Strikersport."

"Then you do not know that this well is said to have great healing qualities."

"I am an ignorant child and have been told but little," Mudan answered in a way that could have meant either yes or no.

"It still does, of course, but it has been weaker in the last few years. Ever since the foreigners came and took over, it has slowly lost much of its strength." As the crowd moved closer to the well, the old woman followed, forcing Mudan to follow in turn. Seeing the way she moved, slow and painfully, Zhanchi instinctively stepped forward and found McLeod doing the same. They looked at each other ruefully and both allowed the old woman to put her skinny fingers on their arms, to clutch tight with a painful grip.

As they all moved closer to the well, the old woman continued her story. "Bai She, an ancient Immortal from the distant and holy kingdom of Khaitan, is here. In thanks for the refuge he received when he was injured, he has blessed its waters. He has told the priests that he will not stay long, but while he remains, he will gift the waters with as much of his power as he can."

That explained matters more than adequately. Belief, especially fresh, new, belief, was a powerful force and Zhanchi suspected someone of making use of that power to grant the waters what they would not ordinarily have. He wondered if this Bai She was a sorcerer using that belief to serve his own ends or a charlatan looking for attention. Khaitan, after all, was just a legend. No lush and fertile kingdom nested in the desert between Tai Shan and Kunlun. Just dreary dust and death. As for why there were so many people at the well—that was the genius behind the ruse. By claiming the change was temporary, the person behind this had ensured as many people as possible would come.

When they reached the well Zhanchi saw the man sitting on the edge. He almost spoke, recognizing him immediately, but realized this was neither the place, nor the time, to mention that he'd met this man, with much shorter hair and far less elaborate clothes, the day before. No one would believe him.

Today the blind man wore silver and white robes and his waist-length hair was bound up in dozens and dozens of fine braids and chains that chimed softly every time he moved. The music reminded Zhanchi of something, a ceremony from his childhood, but he couldn't quite remember what it'd been for. Something to do with snakes, he thought. Snakes and rivers. The man's name, meaning White Snake, was more than appropriate.

The man raised his face as the old woman came closer and he smiled in a way that made his haughty features turn gentle. "Child," he said. "You have tasted my waters before. You know there's little they can do for you now."

"I know, Lord of the Hidden River," she said, in a way that suggested she knew far more than she'd told Mudan, "But it has been long and long since I was permitted to visit your land and I wished one last taste before the end."

Bai She sighed and lifted a single droplet from the well beside him. "For what you and yours have done for me," he said tenderly, "I give what I can. Your time will come soon and quiet, as you desire." He allowed the droplet to fall into her open mouth.

The old woman bowed and released her hold on Zhanchi and McLeod, leaving them with more spring to her step than there'd been before. Now the stranger turned to Zhanchi and his companions, wearing his most distant and most haughty expression. To McLeod he said, "You may drink if you wish, but it will do little for you. Your faith belongs to the one you love and to no other."

"I... think I understand."

"Good. Take care of her and she will take care of you."

The white haired man turned his attention on Zhanchi. "You do not know it but you already belong to another."

Zhanchi wished he could have said the same as McLeod. "I don't know what you mean."

"You will. Or at least you'd better. Learn to recognize him, before he loses patience with you."

Before Zhanchi could say another word, the man pointed off towards the temple behind them. "Mudan, your God awaits you, and the thing you guard, most impatiently. I suggest you go to him before he comes to us."

They stared at him and he made a shooing motion. "Well? Am I speaking Russian? Run along. Now."

It was Mudan who acted first, catching hold of McLeod's wrist and dragging him along behind her. Perforce, Zhanchi followed, with Shen not far behind.

((((

Conall couldn't help looking back as Mudan dragged him away. "That's the man from yesterday," he said and knew how foolish he sounded. Who could forget someone dressed like that? Especially when he was surrounded on all sides by those odd shadowy figures that seemed to be both part of him and separate.

One of those shadows waved at him in imitation of its source's shooing gesture and he faced forward, aware of the look Zhanchi was giving him. "Yes, it's him. Didn't expect to see him dressed up like Madam White Snake, but I'd know that arrogant smirk anywhere."

Puzzled, Conall said, "Dressed up? Like Madam White Snake?"

"Well, not exactly. I don't think there's a theater in Shanghai can afford that much real silver. But he could have stepped right off an opera stage. And there still aren't that many women actors, so…."

Conall remembered Mudan telling him the story of the two lovers denied marriage because the one was an immortal serpent spirit and the other a human man. It'd been part of how she'd tried to persuade him that the two of them could never be, though he still thought the whole thing foolish. But something else confused him. "I don't understand what you mean about his costume. That's the same thing he was wearing yesterday."

Mudan halted suddenly and stared at him. "What?"

"He's dressed exactly the same as he was yesterday," Conall repeated.

"No, he's not," Zhanchi protested. "He was dressed like a gangster yesterday. White suit, white tie, white shoes. And his hair was short. Not all braids and chains."

Slowly, Shen said, "Do you see through illusions?"

Conall blinked, still puzzled. "I don't know. If I see through them, I wouldn't know they were there in the first place."

"An accurate assessment of such a talent. Allow me to test it." Shen lifted his hand, and asked, "All of you. Tell me what you see."

"A white tiger." "A flowery dragon." "Nothing." Mudan, Zhanchi and Conall said at once.

The driver considered Conall thoughtfully. "A useful but dangerous talent, child. You must be careful, because there are those who would not have their illusions broken."

Remembering Wugong, Conall realized why he'd been so confused that first meeting. The man must have hidden his centipedes behind some illusion. Before he could say so, something like a pair of cold hands pressed at his back. Mudan and Zhanchi jumped as well and he realized they were being pushed by shadowy figures whose resemblance to that white haired man was just visible in the bright noon light.

"I think we're being told to keep moving. It seems neither Bai She, nor your God, will wait much longer," Shen said.

Mudan agreed and they hurried past the big main building of the temple to a small nook off in one corner. It almost didn't seem real and Mudan hesitated in front of it for a moment. "You don't have to come with me. He can be difficult to deal with for His Priests. It's much harder for outsiders."

"I will remain here," Shen agreed. "I have nothing to tell him at the moment. You should stay with me, Zhanchi."

"But...."

"Don't wander into another's territory when you don't yet know your own," Shen said firmly and to Conall's surprise, Zhanchi obeyed, going to sit on a bench.

Mudan looked at Conall, obviously intending to tell him to wait but he spoke before she could. "I'm coming with you." This wasn't the first time Conall had faced her God and though Meng Huang Hsiang scared the life out of him he wouldn't leave Mudan. She gazed at him and to his surprise, instead of showing exasperation as she had before, she took his hand and led him forward.

((((

At first the interior of Meng Huang Hsiang's shrine seemed like any other small shrine to a nearly forgotten God. Indeed, Mudan suspected it didn't belong to her God at all. It would be like him to drop in uninvited and make himself at home. Hopefully the shrine's proper owner wouldn't take offense.

As they passed the doorway Mudan felt a shudder in reality and knew they were no longer in Shanghai. Indeed, not only had they left Shanghai but this was not what the world called China, nor even part of the world at all. This was His shrine in Khaitan, the great ancient cavern in the depths of that kingdom's Pamir Mountains.

Hot breezes warred with icy ones, spinning around Mudan and Conall and making her feel as if she were coming down with a cold or worse. No surprise, that. Meng Huang Hsiang was the God of fever dreams. It was a side effect one had to expect and accept.

The further they walked along the narrow path towards Meng Huang Hsiang's statue at the far end of the room, the more Mudan had to keep her thoughts carefully controlled. She could sense Him touching her mind, forcing her to contemplate things she didn't like to face. That too was to be expected and she neither fought nor surrendered. Beside her, Conall muttered something under his breath, a denial; of what, she didn't know.

Memories flooded Mudan's mind, showing her the last time they'd entered His shrine together. It'd been brave, terribly brave, of Conall to dare such a thing. Oh, he hadn't known what he'd face when he came in after her, but by the time he'd reached the altar, he'd been shaking in his shoes and covered in cold sweat. She'd had to nurse him back to health for days.

Memory of Conall's voice whispering as he asked her to marry him echoed through the great hall mockingly. "Before your God I swear and promise to stand at your side and be your partner in love and in life." It'd been an oath she dared not acknowledge, nor accept.

The air seemed to flutter and shift and Mudan found herself watching Conall as he worked on the metal sheathing the great gold dragon he was building for the Lunar New Years parade. She would turn eighteen just before the year ended and while the coming year belonged to the wood dog, her father wished to acknowledge her with a float celebrating her animal; the fire dragon. "Chinese dragons do not breathe fire, Mr. McLeod," she scolded, as Conall tested the device he'd added to cause what appeared to be a gout of flame to erupt from the device's mouth.

"But your birth year was fire dragon," he argued, turning to look at her, entirely unaware of his appearance, with his shirt all twisted and his shaggy red hair sticking out in all directions. "Isn't it? And I told you to call me Conall."

"It does not matter. You are not a carpenter because you are a wood tiger. The element belongs to the year, not the animal."

He cocked his head at her, looking strangely innocent. "All the dragons I've ever heard of breathe fire."

"Western dragons, maybe. But not Chinese."

"Well, if you insist." He jumped down to tower over her, smiling in a way that set her pulse racing. "I'll do whatever you'd like. It's your gift, after all. Besides, fire chars wood every time. Chinese dragons may not breathe fire, but you, my love, do."

Once again the memory changed. Mudan's father, telling her gently, "I do not approve, I am not pleased, and I do not permit. You must not see that boy again. Not here. Not now."

"But father."

"No. I am your father and I will have you safe. The old ways are best. Stay apart and do not love outsiders, especially when they are white men. Americans do not accept those of our blood. Their laws deny us and would have us leave. Marry him and the wrath of his kin may come down upon both your heads."

Mudan didn't care. Law, no matter what authority commanded it, she regarded as any proper descendent of Ching Shi should; as a guideline to be ignored when it inconvenienced one. Parental authority—especially when that parent ruled the Jeen Loon—on the other hand, was another question entirely. Unwillingly and with great regret, she had accepted her father's orders and obeyed.

Mudan's ears buzzed and she realized she'd been so lost in memories that she hadn't noticed when they'd reached the altar. A great statue stood atop it, the original version of the smaller one in her temple back home. A beautiful young man garbed in a loose robe, rode a white tiger backwards. His mad eyes watched her and His mad voice echoed in her ears, babbling what seemed to be nonsense. It took time and effort to truly comprehend His words and even when you thought understood them, you risked misinterpreting His intent.

"Come to me, child. Why are you not listening to me?"

"Lord," she said. "I wish to. I yearn to. But I don't understand."

"Talking to you?"

"Am I"

"Who do you think I mean."

The sentences were spoken in rapid succession and it took Mudan several moments to realize what they meant. "It's not me you want?" It couldn't be Conall. She was almost certain her God liked Conall but by no stretch of the imagination did he belong to the God. The warmth around her wrist pulsed and she remembered her bracelet. Guessing it was Meng Huang Hsiang's target, she took it off. "Go to Him," she ordered, feeling it quiver with what might be fear.

It shuddered and the little dragon head shook like a small child refusing to obey.

"Father. Mother. Parent. Come, runaway."

Once again it argued silently, trying to crawl up the sleeve of her jacket. That only exasperated her and she very gently pulled it back out and held it by the nape of the neck. "I do not understand all of this," she said. "But I understand enough. Meng Huang Hsiang would have you face Him and Meng Huang Hsiang is your Lord as well as mine. Obey Him, little one, as I obey my father."

That got a chuckle from her God, and she heard her father's voice in her head repeating what old Chang had said. "You must not see him again. Not here. Not now."

It was true she'd disobeyed, but in a way she hadn't. She'd not been permitted to see Conall back home. Shanghai was most definitely not home. For that matter, that was in the past, its 'now' lost to time. Once again Meng Huang Hsiang chuckled. Most Gods would decry sophistry, but He tended to approve. "Besides," He said, as clear as He ever could be. "I rather like that boy of yours. He makes pretty pretties. Like that little train he tried to bribe me with."

Puzzled, Mudan turned to look at Conall. "Train?" she repeated. "Bribe?"

Conall flushed bright red. "I brought it to him back in August—when everyone was busy with the Hungry Ghost Festival," he told her. "I thought it'd help if your God was on our side."

Reflecting that Conall was fortunate that such games suited her God only too well, Mudan just said, "He was never anywhere else but there." She turned her attention on her little dragonet. "Now. You. Do as you're told."

Sulkily, it obeyed, and the God held it in His hand for a long moment. "You should not have run. Now the greater part of you is lost and you are weakened. What will you do to rectify this?" There was silence, but Mudan guessed the dragonet answered by Meng Huang Hsiang's next words. "See that you do, little one. Go with your mistress now and give her no trouble. Mudan?"

"Yes, Lord?"

"I gift him to you. Find the part of him he's lost and he will be a weapon of great power."

"Thank you, my Lord." Mudan let the little dragon wrap itself around her wrist again and felt it wriggle contentedly when she stroked its head.

"One more thing. Filial piety is good and right, but fathers do not always know what is best for their children. Times change and those who do not change with them will be lost beneath history."

Mudan bowed. "I do not pretend to comprehend your meaning, but I will think on it and try."

"See that you do. Now, go back. You have a great deal of work ahead of you."

A moment later they were standing inside a shrine to one of the Taoist Immortals—Zhang Guolao, riding backwards on his donkey. Before she could say anything, the sound of screaming outside drew their attention and they hurried into the courtyard, just in time to see a huge black beast fly overhead. Its tattered wings dripped water as it veered and struggled to stay in the air. As it flew southwest it roared furiously, flames jetting from its mouth.

"See," Conall couldn't seem to help saying. "Didn't I tell you? Dragons breathe fire."

Chapter Nine
Foreign Planes are Being Imported in Large Numbers

Fukushima dragged herself and Kurumata out of the water some distance away from where they'd gone in. "I will kill them. I will bomb their lair, their city, their entire country!" Kurumata swore as he struggled out of the water. "How dare they use such weapons? How dare they attack my men? How dare they attack me?!"

To shut him up, Fukushima said, "I'd heard rumors of that beast before. It is as terrible as they say. Your men died bravely."

"That beast? That was nothing but a delusion! Soong's men must have filled the air with hallucinogens, no doubt stolen from our research at *Tōgō* Unit. All they needed to do was confuse my men and burn them to death with flame throwers."

Fukushima knew too well what research Kurumata meant. *Zhongma* Fortress, or Unit *Tōgō*, had been part of a secret division that had experimented on Chinese prisoners. Some of those prisoners had escaped late last year, revealing what was being done there. She smiled grimly to herself, being one of the few who knew why the fortress had been closed.

Oblivious to his rescuer, Kurumata waved his hands, screaming imprecations at a happily empty sky. He might believe that dragon had been a vision brought on by some drug, but Fukushima was certain he was wrong. It was either that or accept she'd gone mad and she wasn't ready to do that.

They were fortunate Soochow Creek was as silty as it was. She'd felt the monster strike the water after they'd escaped and had desperately held her breath to stay below the surface, praying it wouldn't find her. They'd been fortunate. She'd been right to think the monster uncomfortable in water. She'd felt the river warming where it crawled, and one brief rise for air had allowed her to hear steam hissing off its body as it searched. Then, unable to remain submerged, it'd taken flight, muttering its own curses as it went.

Still, she wouldn't argue the point. "I suggest you regroup. See if any of your men survived. I doubt Soong Kou or Feng Wugong are still there. As for that woman, Zhi Lin, she is no longer of any use."

Now he was eyeing her suspiciously. "Just who are you? How did you get here? What were you doing in that place?"

"I am Fukushima Hikaru, Lieutenant. As for how I got there and why; you do not have the clearance to be told anything of my mission." She straightened her outfit, regretting that the material was not likely to survive the soaking unharmed. "Now, I'm ordering you to go find your men and return to your base to report."

The look on Kurumata's face went from distrust, to uncertainty to a momentary look of raw panic. For a moment she thought it was her avowed position as an agent that had elicited the reaction but then she realized he was staring up the bank behind her.

Annoyed at her inattention, Fukushima turned to see a dozen British soldiers, all eyeing her, and her soaking wet clothes, with bemused expressions. "Well now," the obvious leader, a rangy sandy-haired fellow with a thick mustache, said. "I'm not one for cliché, but I have to ask: What's all this then?"

((((

Wugong dragged Zhi Lin to her feet. "If you can't run," he said in a hard voice, "you burn. I'm not carrying you."

"Fair enough." He wasn't surprised when she stood on her own and pulled the bandages covering her face away. He'd thought she'd been pretending from the moment he'd seen her. "Which way? And what was that damned thing?"

Packing his papers into his briefcase quickly, Soong snapped. "None of your business, assassin. If we told you anything it'd go straight to the wrong ears."

Reflecting his boss was probably right, Wugong led the way out of the office to the far end from the raging fire. This building was finished. No one owned it and no one cared enough to do more than keep its flames from spreading. It was a good thing they had a mobile operation. All they would have to do was head to another hideout and they could set up shop again.

"It nearly killed me yesterday," Zhi Lin complained. "Don't I at least have the right to know what it was?"

"It's our ally and a dangerous one to cross," Soong told her. "That's all you need to know."

"How did Chen keep him from eating you?" Wugong asked, to distract her from asking questions they didn't want to answer.

They were down the ladder by now and headed out the door. Wugong could hear the sound of people shouting and hoped they could get past the crowd without anyone recognizing them. An illusion spell would be useful right now, but his magic only worked on centipedes.

It took Zhi Lin a minute before she answered Wugong's question. "Is that his name? Chen? He just grinned when I asked." At both Wugong and Soong's silence she continued, saying, "It was dark and I couldn't see the fight. All I know is that he was on that monster's back and he forced it to land before it could get me. After that, I heard something like a whip swinging in the air."

Somehow, Wugong doubted a whip could do the sort of damage Raud had taken. Not that he expected Chen to explain. That was a man who kept his own secrets. Well enough, he thought. Chen wasn't important. They didn't need a thief right now. Just someone to capture McLeod and kill Striker's woman. It was too bad, though, that Zhi Lin's mistake with the *tun* fish meant she was no longer useful in Sir Bruce's house. If Raud resented Sir Bruce being poisoned, it was certain the man himself must be furious.

They continued through the streets of the industrial district and into the slum and from there into Chapei. There was a hidden cellar there that had become second among Soong's preferred hideouts. They'd nearly arrived when Zhi Lin, who had apparently decided to stay with them for the moment, hissed and pulled Wugong back. "Look out," she whispered as Soong stopped a foot or so ahead of them to glare at her. "No further."

Half-expecting her to be panicking over the fact that there were planes circling over the city now, Wugong started to pull his arm free of her grip. Then he saw what she was looking at and groaned. Several men from Soong's gang were walking down the street, looking like they were on a stroll, and they weren't alone. The three men were companioned by some big, muscular, Westerners. By their short, short, hair, light skin and eyes and their general demeanor, they were soldiers. By their accents, overheard when one of Soong's men tripped, they were American.

That alone was bad enough. Worse was the realization that one soldier carried an all too familiar bottle. The Americans had their treasure and were taking it with them.

《《《

"LOOK OUT," SHE WHISPERED...

Kurumata Katashi was the angriest he'd been since he'd been assigned to this wretched city. The last time he'd been so furious was when those damned Chinese had taken advantage of the commander's kindness to escape. He hadn't taken the blame for that fiasco, however, but for what came of it. Those few prisoners who'd survived and made it to safety had revealed the experiments being performed at *Tōgō* unit, shocking minds too tender to deal with reality.

Even that wouldn't have been Kurumata's fault. But he and his commander ought to have realized the consequences of such news getting out. Even now, he wasn't sure who'd flown the unmarked bi-plane past the Manchurian border in broad daylight to attack the camp, bombing every guard house and barrack to pieces without injuring a single Chinese prisoner.

Whoever he was, Kurumata was torn between admiration for the pilot's flying skills and fury at his temerity. He'd been in one of the towers at the time, had even seen the plane's pilot and his companion in one brief, terrifying moment as the plane had passed so close the wing nearly brushed Kurumata from his perch. He still woke in a cold sweat at the memory, seeing the pilot's broad grin beneath his goggles as he waved insolently, his companion turned the other way to throw another bomb.

They'd closed *Tōgō* Unit after that and Kurumata hadn't been invited to join Unit 731. Instead he'd been assigned to Shanghai, a decadent city full of decadent foreigners, decadent Chinese and—worse—decadent Japanese. Poets. Writers. Artists. Musicians. All the dregs of Japan's so-called creative community who'd found their way of life made them unwelcome back home.

The only positive was the gratifying respect he received from the Westerners of Shanghai. The rest of the world was beginning to understand his people's power. The British, fools though they were, treated him with the wary respect he knew he deserved. Japan's recent bombing of Chapei to rubble had had a most beneficial effect.

Right now, however, he was receiving no respect at all. Having been seen escaping the burning remains of the cotton mill had given the British authorities an excuse to hold him. The fact that he was a citizen of Japan and a member of its military wasn't enough to convince them to let him go.

He paced in the small room, pausing only to look through the window and watch an RAF plane fly past. They'd been at it ever since the fire, circling over the city as if searching for something. If he didn't know better, he'd have thought it was that so-called dragon of Soong's.

What he'd seen had to be a hallucination brought on by some drug. It couldn't possibly have been a real dragon. Such creatures, Eastern or Western, didn't exist. Kurumata tried to ignore the still voice at the back of his mind that pointed out that Soong had had no opportunity to drug him.

The door to the room opened and the British soldier who'd brought him in for questioning entered. "Lieutenant Kurumata, I apologize for taking so long, but since you didn't have any identification on you, we had to send for someone to confirm your identity." The man with him, Kurumata's superior Shikawa Nori, looked on Kurumata with little favor. "Captain Shikawa? Is this your man?"

"Regrettably." Shikawa barely gave Kurumata another glance. "I may take him with me?"

"Could I ask him one question?"

"Asking is, as the Americans say, free. I offer no guarantees of an answer," Shikawa replied coolly.

"Then did your men find that engine Soong's selling?"

At Shikawa's slight nod, Kurumata told the man, "Everything happened so fast that I couldn't tell who was an ally or an enemy." That didn't really answer the question, but it was the precise truth. If there was an engine of any sort in that warehouse it'd either been removed before his men could find it or destroyed in the fire. Either way, he didn't know where it was.

The British commander sighed. "Well enough. This whole mess just gets more tangled every minute." He eyed Shikawa. "You know we want it. We know you want it. The Nationalists want it. The Communists want it. There are Americans out there right now, looking for it. For all I know Argentina will be after it next. And all for a thing we don't even know is real."

That startled Kurumata and he shot a look at Shikawa, who'd told him on no uncertain terms that the Soong engine was vital to Japan's effort to claim its proper, supreme, place over the East. If Shikawa had any thoughts on the matter, however, he said not a word. Instead, he bowed. "The future is, by its nature, not real. All we can do is move forward into it. Kurumata, come with me."

They left the room and Kurumata made certain there was no one near before asking Shikawa, "What about Fukushima?" He didn't like the woman but he did owe her his life.

"Fukushima is to remain in British custody." Shikawa smiled. "I like to have ears on the inside and how else shall I find out what these fools learn about that engine?"

As they headed back to headquarters it occurred to Kurumata to wonder, but not to ask, exactly how Fukushima would get any word of what she learned out of prison, given she'd learned anything. It never did to pry too deeply into one's superior's plans.

Chapter Ten
Superstitions Among the Uneducated Chinese Run Rampant

Mudan's expression was a familiar one and Zhanchi was glad it was aimed at McLeod. Her dark eyes were wide and her thin lips tight as if to keep from shouting. Zhanchi's mother glared at him the same way the last time she'd caught him folding paper planes to send flying out into the gorge beside their house in Guangzhou.

McLeod was either oblivious or unintimidated, convincing Zhanchi that the American was too ignorant, and possibly too stupid, to recognize danger staring him in the face. Instead of cowering from Mudan's glare as any sane man ought, McLeod simply spread his hands wide, "Well, it looked like a dragon to me."

"That doesn't make it a Chinese dragon," Zhanchi couldn't help retorting. "They don't have wings and they don't breathe fire."

"How do they fly, then? For that matter, if they don't breathe fire, what do they breathe?"

Mudan's eye twitched but the thing that stopped Zhanchi from responding was the soft growl behind him. Shen had been so quiet for the last few minutes that Zhanchi had all but forgotten he was there. Now the cabbie was making a noise that reminded Zhanchi of one of the small but ferocious dogs his mother's mother kept at her side. When Zhanchi looked, he realized Shen's upper lip was curled back from strangely sharp canines as he glared in the direction the dragon had gone. "Would you like to find out?" he asked softly in a dialect of Chinese that Zhanchi had only learned at his father's insistence. He'd never heard anyone speak it before.

Bai She suddenly emerged from a particularly black patch of shadow, his braids jingling softly as he moved. Gently, he put a hand on Shen's shoulder and murmured in the same tongue, "No, young one. This is neither the time nor place to reveal yourself."

Ordinarily, Zhanchi would have questioned Bai She's calling Shen 'young one' when, at least by face, they looked the same age, but something warned him to silence. Zhanchi was beginning to realize just how much of the magical world were bringing their forces to bear on Shanghai. He'd no interest in his family's traditional occupation as mystics and priests, but he'd had no choice but to learn the rudiments. The white-haired man had to be an Immortal after all, though which of the hundreds of possibilities was something Zhanchi couldn't guess.

Shen growled under his breath as several RAF planes flew overhead, following the path the dragon had taken. Now it was Zhanchi's turn to be agitated. A dragon, a foreign dragon, had been bad enough. Now British planes were flying over his land in pursuit and the only thing he wanted was to be in the air himself. His fingers twitched helplessly as he contemplated the possibilities of following suit.

Bai She put his hand on Zhanchi's shoulder as well. "Don't consider it. The airfield is nowhere near and even if it was, their planes lack the weapons needed to fight that monster." This time he spoke in Mandarin.

"I didn't need weapons for *Tōgō* Unit," Zhanchi snapped. "Just the judicious application of dynamite." It was an admission he shouldn't make. There was only one other person who knew about it and she had ample reason to keep her silence.

"Dynamite not strong enough for that, I think," McLeod said suddenly in his halting and atrocious Chinese, proving that he understood enough of the conversation to know what Zhanchi wanted to do. "Something bigger, better. Machine gun, maybe?"

"No." Mudan said firmly. "There will be no dragon hunt. Besides, it appears to have escaped the British. Already they return to base. Searching for it now would only reveal what you do not wish revealed. It is better for us to return to the others. By now their foolish game is surely over and we will be expected to go with Sir Bruce and the others."

Zhanchi yearned to say she was wrong. Yet he knew he had to obey Murtagh. He didn't like his employer, at times he actively hated the man, but without Murtagh's sponsorship he would still be sitting around the airfield, waiting for the off chance that one of the American pilots might be too ill, or too lazy, to fly. Waiting for a chance to rise that never seemed to come.

Knowing all that and knowing, too, that he didn't have a plane to chase a dragon with anyway, Zhanchi agreed unwillingly.

(((

As they left *Jing'an* temple a dozen settlement police, led by a discontented looking British officer, rushed up the street. At first Mudan wasn't sure why the police had come; there was no sign of trouble nearby. Only when the leader started shouting angrily did she understand. The sudden and mysterious—at least to the authorities—gathering of native Chinese had worried the man's superiors and that in turn worried him.

Mudan wasn't concerned over Shanghai's attempt at crowd control. She'd no doubt those involved with the gathering would fade away quickly, evading arrest and the officer's threats of violence with the ease of long practice. Those who didn't would learn to do so better next time, or so she hoped.

What concerned Mudan was the small group of men walking east along the road. Some were Chinese, poorly dressed and poorly groomed, but they were companioned by several larger men whose civilian clothing couldn't conceal their military bearing. She wasn't sure if they were British or American but it hardly mattered. What was important was the thing one man carried. A glass jar half-filled with a silvery substance and capped with a peculiar device. Somehow she knew, without being sure how, that it was the rest of her small companion's whole.

As Mudan recognized the jar's contents, her bracelet suddenly slid off her arm and gave chase, rushing past the big policeman and causing him to stare wildly after it. His expression said he was quickly deciding that he had not, and could not, have seen what he thought he saw. Just as well. They didn't need additional trouble.

Not wanting to let her bracelet escape, Mudan headed after it. "Conall, wait here with Zhanchi," she started to say before she realized both men were following behind her closely. "You should stay put," she grumbled, although she wasn't sorry they'd come after her. For that matter, she was relieved to find Shen as well. He was, at the very least, a sorcerer and possibly more. Still, she told them, "You all should."

"No," Shen said. "My uncle may have given the task to you, but it is also mine. Besides, you'll need help, and Bai She is still too ill to act."

"I don't suppose you could tell me what that bracelet is?" Conall added as he walked beside her, carefully allowing her to remain a step or so ahead despite his longer stride. "Aside from obviously being magic, that is?"

"Hey! You four!" That was the police officer, who'd decided their behavior was suspicious. "Where are you going?" He made a gesture to his men to block the path. "What are you up to?"

It was Conall who answered, instinctively recognizing that this man would take anything a Chinese person said as either misdirection or lie. "We're just taking a walk, sir. No harm in that, is there?"

"Did you have something to do with that crowd?" By now the others had dispersed, fading into the woodwork as Mudan had expected. Frustrated by their escape, the officer was turning his ire on the only ones available. Not even Conall being white helped, since he was obviously and unabashedly companioning himself with heathen Chinese.

Before Conall could offer a suitable answer, someone screamed. It was a terrible sound, made the more so by coming from the throat of one of the big American soldiers. He was waving his hands around wildly as if trying to brush something off.

For a moment Mudan feared her bracelet had attacked the man, then she recognized Wugong and a dozen or so men blocking the Americans' path. Another motion drew her attention and she spotted the Black Jade Fox slipping between two larger men and out of sight. She wondered what he was doing there and if he were enemy or ally this time round. He was her father's friend, but the side he favored first was his own.

"Bloody hell." The British officer turned and, seeing the fight, sent his men to join in.

No longer the center of the policeman's attention, Mudan hesitated only a moment. She still needed to get her bracelet back. "Zhanchi, what magic is it your brother uses?"

"My family are usually beast summoners. Wugong has an affinity with bugs."

"What about you?" Conall asked curiously as they all headed for the fight. "Can you do anything?"

"Not really. I like anything that flies, so birds would have been the obvious choice. But I wanted to fly, myself, not through a pet."

Shen said what Mudan was thinking before she could. "This is not the time."

"Always time to learn," Conall retorted as he pulled a centipede off the soldier's neck. "Is there anything to be done about the poison?" he asked, holding the thing behind the head until Shen took it and crushed it in a gloved hand.

"One bite's survivable. Two would be dangerous. Three would kill most men." Zhanchi answered, catching hold of another centipede and giving it to Shen.

Ignoring the others to search out Wugong himself, Mudan found the gangster fighting with the fellow holding the jar. That one was a good fighter and Mudan guessed Wugong didn't dare use his centipedes on him for fear he might drop the jar.

The metal inside bounced and sloshed and Mudan caught a glimpse of an eye looking at her pleadingly. Its expression was exactly the same as her bracelet's and she knew for certain it was what Meng Huang Hsiang had commanded her to rescue.

Joining the fight, Mudan blocked Wugong's strike and received a glare of pure fury. "Make yourself up as one of us all you want," he snapped in English. "I know you for what you are."

"You know nothing," she answered in Cantonese, knowing it for his native dialect. As he swung at her she stepped back out of his way while the man with the jar tried to kick him in the side. "But it is not my business to instruct you. If a man does not heed his parents, how can this low born daughter of the sea hope to plumb your ignorance?"

Furiously, Wugong flung one of his centipedes at her, but this time she was ready. Knowing one of those trying to capture Conall was a sorcerer, she'd taken to carrying a fan carefully embedded with spells to dissipate magic. Before the insect reached her, she drew the fan from her sleeve and flipped it open, brushing the centipede aside as she spun. Then her elbow took Wugong in the chest and she swung around again, kicking him in the face with her heel.

Whatever he tried to call her was incomprehensible. His teeth had been loosened by her kick and the blood from his nose streamed into his mouth. She was about to press her attack when whistles blasted loudly. The police had called for reinforcements.

Wugong would have continued the fight if another man hadn't grabbed him. "Come."

"But, Soong! She...."

"Later."

Then they were gone and dozens of uniformed men were pouring into the street from either direction. As Mudan looked around she realized the American with the jar had disappeared from sight. The only ones left were Conall, Zhanchi, Shen, two of the American soldiers and a few dozen gangsters rolling around on the ground groaning. She moved to join Conall and as the police gathered around them, wondered where her bracelet had gone and what to do about finding it.

(((

Conall wasn't surprised to be dragged off to the local police station. Separated from Mudan and questioned, he said nothing about Gods, Immortals or little metal dragons. He and his companions had been sightseeing, that was all. No one could take offense at an American walking one of the most famous streets of Shanghai to view *Jing'an* temple. He even brought out his guide book to show the officer questioning him the paragraph suggesting a visit.

"That's not the thing, now is it? The question is why you got involved in that fight at all." Officer Croydon demanded, straightening an already painfully straight notepad and adjusting his pen to what was apparently the precisely correct position to his upper right.

"Well, fellow Americans were being attacked. I figured I'd at least help get them to safety. I didn't intend to be involved in the fight itself." Indeed, for the most part he'd spent his time dragging the unconscious men out of the way, while Zhanchi and Shen had protected him. There'd been another man, that skinny little fellow Mudan had called the Black Jade Fox, but he'd slipped Mudan's bracelet into Conall's hand and disappeared, telling him to return it to Mudan.

That same bracelet now resided around his wrist, its tiny claws tapping impatiently whenever it could get away with moving without anyone else noticing. It wanted this nonsense over as much as Conall. He stroked its head lightly in hopes of quieting it and felt it purr at his touch.

Croydon's cynical expression said he'd heard such stories all too often before. Noticing something about the frame hanging beside his desk, he stood up and adjusted it. "If you weren't Sir Bruce's guests, I'd lock you up and send you packing back to America. Especially when you're caught associating with the likes of Mudan Chang. You shouldn't walk out with the daughters of suspected smugglers like Cheh Chang, you realize?"

"Mudan is an honest and law-abiding American citizen," Conall answered, "As for her father, I've done engineering work for him in the past and have never found him to be anything other than honorable." That didn't answer the question but he wouldn't admit what he knew, or guessed, about the Chang family or its holdings. What he'd said was still the honest truth. He liked the old scoundrel, even though Mr. Chang had denied him Mudan's hand in marriage when Conall had asked.

"And you had nothing to do with that crowd at the Bubbling Well? Someone told us that you seemed familiar with the charlatan who'd taken up shop there."

This time it was the man's chair that needed to be moved to exactly the right angle. Conall couldn't help shifting his own seat to a position slightly off from the one beside it, just to see what Croydon would do. "We were interested in why there was a crowd. And a lady needed help to reach the well. If you know we spoke to the fellow I'm sure someone told you that much too."

"And why follow his instructions? Was he passing some contraband by hiding it in that shrine?" Croydon's lips tightened and he once more rose from his desk, this time to readjust the chair beside Conall so that they matched again.

Innocently pretending he hadn't noticed, Conall asked, "How do you know we didn't go to pay our respects?"

"Because, you young idiot, it's a load of ignorant superstitious codswollop! Hell, even those peasants don't really believe any of it. They just do it to have an excuse for behaving the way they do! You can tell they're all just laughing up those big sleeves of theirs, every time they insist on time off for some ritual or to run through the streets with those damned so-called lion dancers, getting in everyone's way and making a fuss!"

Conall felt the bracelet shift and carefully put his hand over it to remind it to behave. "I wouldn't dare say what anyone believes, but I see no reason to be disrespectful." He nudged his chair sideways a tad, so it was once more out of line with the other.

With a dark and angry look, Officer Croydon growled, "Is that the best you have to say?"

"Yes," Conall agreed amiably, knowing his frequent and sometimes deliberate appearance of clumsy distractibility was—for once—an asset. No one, especially this British police officer, clearly obsessed by neatness and order, would believe Conall was engaged in any form of deception. Or, rather, someone like Croydon would be certain that any lie Conall attempted would be obvious and inept.

Slowly Croydon looked Conall over and concluded he'd get nothing of use from the American simpleton. "Fine, then. If that's all you have to say, and given I have nothing to hold you on, you're free to go."

That said, Croydon rose and—after 'fixing' the two guest chairs without comment—escorted Conall out of his office to the waiting area. "If you and your friends plan on staying in Shanghai much longer," he told Conall as they waited for Mudan and the others to join them, "you need to present yourselves to the American Consulate. They'll want to know how long you're going to be here."

Not said, but implied, was a distinct desire for Conall's stay to be a short one. Fortunately, Conall didn't need to answer, for that was when Mudan came out to join him. She looked as serene as ever, but he could see the mild irritation in her eyes. To alleviate her annoyance, he offered her the bracelet. "It slipped off your arm just before the fight," he told her truthfully, knowing Croydon was listening.

The man's expression was disapproving, a reaction Conall was now inured to, but he didn't object as Mudan took the bracelet with a look that combined relief with obvious delight. Impulsively and gratifyingly, she raised herself up on her tiptoes and kissed his cheek. "You'll have to tell me how you retrieved it, later," she said as he smiled fatuously on her.

Conall would probably have said or done something to embarrass Mudan if Zhanchi and Shen hadn't arrived then. "That," Shen said quietly in Chinese, "was very nearly humiliating."

"They not hurt you?" Conall asked in the same language. Spoken slowly enough for his untrained ears, he could generally understand the language, but he knew his pronunciation was, as Zhanchi had pointed out, execrable. He could never quite get the intonation to match what he'd thought he'd heard.

"No. I am uninjured in anything but my dignity. And we should go quickly. The Hunt will be long since over and we are now very late," Shen turned to the door, and Croydon frowned sharply. As they left the station, Conall noticed the officer speak to one of his men and gesture at Shen.

Wondering what it was about Shen's behavior that had made the officer suspicious, Conall trailed alongside Mudan and hoped there wouldn't be more trouble immediately. They'd had quite enough already.

《《《

Chapter Eleven
The City of Shanghai is Governed by Three Separate Entities

ajor Grant-Merchant was displeased for any number of reasons, not least the fact that he'd been forced to release that Kurumata chap. Now he had to release the girl he and his men had captured as well. Worse, he was releasing her to the silly, horse-mad, upper-class twit she apparently had taken up with. If Lord William Holm didn't have connections at high command, the Major would have happily sent the fellow packing.

"Don't suppose you know if your pilots found that plane they were chasing?" Lord William asked casually as he waited patiently for his mistress' release.

What Grant-Merchant wanted to say was that it wasn't Lord William's business but he knew what his commander would say if he was rude to the damned fool. "No. It disappeared before they could get close." He didn't add that he was almost sure the black plane had been Chinese. Only they would build something to look like some sort of dragon.

Admittedly, the Chinese weren't much on engineering—they needed white men to help them on that count—but he'd bet they had some airstrip hidden somewhere out in the hills to the west of Shanghai. Couldn't be a very big one, though. Someone would have noticed by now. Wherever it was, he'd bet his last paycheck some local warlord was in on the plot. The question was, who? Zhao was a possibility, but he was all the way down in Hanchow. Still, it was rumored he had a small landing strip near his castle.

"I see. Well the damned thing scared the devil out of half the horses at the hunt. Someone should do something about that."

Grant-Merchant rolled his eyes behind Lord William's back. "No doubt, sir."

"I even heard that some of the Chinese are claiming it's some sort of dragon, and not one of theirs."

"No doubt what they want their people to think. You know how superstitious some of those peasants are. They'll believe anything." Funny thing was Grant-Merchant thought Chinese dragons didn't have wings, much less the ability to breathe fire. Annoyed at himself for his own distraction, he countered, "It's rot, pure and simple. Whatever it was, it couldn't possibly be a dragon."

Thoughtfully, staring out the window and looking at the sky, Lord William said softly, "Most likely right on that count. Just wish it hadn't looked so much like one when it dive-bombed the Hunt." The door opened then and Miss Fukushima walked in, accompanied by two of Grant-Merchant's men. "Ah, Hikaru. I was worried about you. I hope you didn't have to wait too long for me?" To Grant-Merchant's irritation, she was remarkably unruffled despite her incarceration.

"No, Billy. I am unhurt. I promise." Listening to her speak, Grant-Merchant was struck by an oddity to her English. It wasn't as pronouncedly accented as most of Hongkew's Japanese residents. If anything, it was almost better than that of some Americans, especially the ones from the southern states. He wondered where she was from but knew better than to ask.

Instead, he said, "Well, that's that, then. Miss Fukushima, have your possessions been returned to you?" It occurred to him that she hadn't been carrying much, an oddity no matter how you looked at it. What was she and how was she involved with that nonsense with Soong and the plane engine his gang were claiming to sell? He'd tried to warn Lord William about her, but the damned fool just smiled and ignored him.

"They have, Major, I thank you." The girl smiled and took Lord William's arm. "Shall we go, Billy? I do so apologize for having taken you away from your much more important pursuits. Did you win the Chase?"

The two of them took their leave of the Major without further discussion and once they were gone, Grant-Merchant turned his attention to Lieutenant Benjamin's report. From the looks of things the pilot was in desperate need of a holiday. It was, after all, the only reason Grant-Merchant could think of for the poor man to be so certain he'd been chasing a real, honest to goodness, dragon.

《《《

Fukushima waited until they'd returned to Lord William's townhouse and they were entirely alone in the man's study before speaking. "I apologize for my failure," she said. "I shouldn't have allowed myself to be captured."

"Better captured by the Major than burned to a crisp," Lord William told her, pouring her a glass of sherry. "Tell me, was that really a dragon? Up until today I was certain all the stories about the Black Dragon of Sunderland were just tall-tales."

"As was I," Fukushima admitted. "But I fear he was entirely too real, and entirely too solid." Not to mention entirely too willing to make use of his terrifying breath. Whatever else Raud was, he was not one to be trifled with. "He didn't like the water, fortunately. I'm certain I, and Kurumata, would have been his dinner otherwise."

Lord William agreed. "And your commander would have lost an excellent agent. Speaking of whom, he and the others will be here soon to discuss the situation. We'll wait until they're here for your report."

It wasn't long after that that Joe Church, officially a clerk of records at the American Consulate, Augustine Gerard, Church's counterpart in the French Consulate and Tsao Tsu, a supposed teak merchant, arrived. It was Church who spoke to Fukushima first. "I hear you had yourself an adventure. You all right, kiddo?"

"I've been far worse," Fukushima stated. "Although I don't think much of my chances of avoiding a cold after swimming in Soochow creek."

"Rumor has it you encountered a legend?" Tsao asked curiously.

"Rumor is, for once, correct," Fukushima agreed unhappily. Honesty demanded she tell them exactly what had happened, despite its seeming impossibility. She hadn't believed dragons existed but she couldn't pretend otherwise, now. The monster was obviously an enemy and somehow allied with Soong and his gang. Her commanding officer and his allies had to understand the danger.

Fortunately, all four men had run into oddities in their time, so while they, too, hadn't believed the legends, they were willing to accept the possibility. Her own commander, Church, regarded Fukushima as entirely reliable, a fact she very much appreciated. Being one of the rare *Nisei* members of the American Secret Service was to always be something of a second-class citizen. That she was also the only woman on the team usually made things worse. Without Church's utmost certainty in her, Fukushima would probably still be relegated to the dull duty of translating Japanese documents and radio transmissions. This despite a training program that only half of her male counterparts had completed.

Once Fukushima finished describing her adventure, Tsao said, "I want to disbelieve, but I was at the Paper Chase this afternoon when that monster dived on us, and I saw enough of it, and its breath, to make me sure I'd be a fool to do so." He sighed. "This is already complicated and growing more so. There are too many players and no certainty who belongs to whom."

"Not to mention the question of that engine," Gerard added. "Is it a thing that is real or is it a trick? You say you saw nothing to prove it either?"

As Fukushima agreed, Church told the others, "My men captured some of Soong's gang when they were escaping the cotton mill. Trouble is, all that lot had was a bottle of something Sergeant Harris said looked like mercury. Even worse, Major Jones, who was carrying the jar, disappeared. No one's sure who took him, either. I won't pretend not to be worried."

The jar would be the same one Fukushima had seen and she wished she understood why it was so important. "Nothing else was found in the remains of the cotton mill?" she asked, hopefully.

"It mostly burned to the ground," Church reported. "The firemen were hard put to keep the flames from spreading. Lucky it was abandoned. Made it more flammable, I guess, but there weren't any workers to be killed."

"True. It is, of all things, a small favor but one to be grateful for." Gerard sipped his whiskey and continued, "But it is the engine that is of greatest importance to us. We must find out what it is and what it can do."

Fukushima agreed. "Our best chance to get close to it is McLeod. It can't be a coincidence that an engineer of his caliber is here in Shanghai, staying at the house of the most senior partner of the group buying the engine."

"And," Gerard suggested, "Perhaps we can convince him that it's in everyone's best interests if he assists us in this matter. An engine like this would be the changer of games on so very many levels. It is not a thing to be trusted in the hands of men who wish to use it only for profit."

Since that was the prime reason Church had formed this unlikely alliance between their four secret services; American, British, Chinese and French he was most definitely in agreement. Which, naturally, meant Fukushima was as well. "I'll see what I can do about getting him on board with us," she said.

"You'll have a chance tonight," Lord William told her. "Sir Bruce has invited me, and thus yourself, to the Eastern Star. You'll have to get him away from Miss Chang, though." At Fukushima's raised brow, Lord William explained, "She has connections with the Jeen Loon. It's quite possible they're also sticking their fingers into the pie. Best not give her an opportunity to pull out the plum."

Although Fukushima suspected Mudan was keeping an eye on McLeod for other reasons entirely, she agreed. "If someone can distract her, I'll do

" NOTHING ELSE WAS FOUND IN THE REMAINS OF THE COTTON MILL?" SHE ASKED HOPEFULLY.

my best to speak privately to McLeod." Beyond that she made no promises. The man might seem absent-minded and bewildered, but she'd noticed a sharp and observant mind behind those vague blue eyes. Not to mention an obstinacy that would make changing his mind a herculean task for any but the strongest of wills.

(((

Wugong watched his boss sit silently behind the mahogany desk in the back office of the Eastern Star, staring through the two-way mirror across from him. Beyond lay the wide open floor of the nightclub's main room, but Soong was paying it no mind. Whatever he was thinking had nothing to do with the preparations for the evening. Wugong was almost certain Soong wasn't even seeing the big, crisp and well starched tablecloths being spread over the tables, or the chairs being decorated with fresh wide ribbons of red satin.

On the dais, a small band of German Jews were practicing, their singer, a pretty, vivacious Japanese woman called Manuela, danced around in front of them, her expression showing just how much she enjoyed the job. Wugong could just hear the woman's voice singing something about being in heaven but not much more.

Soong spoke suddenly. "And no one knows where the American went?"

"One of our men says he thought he saw some of the priests grab him. I had them search the temple—politely of course—but there was no sign of anything strange." Wugong wondered what they were going to do. Without the jar of magical quicksilver, they had nothing at all to sell the British-Oriental Consortium.

Properly controlled, the living metal could continuously circulate itself through an engine's workings, driving its pistons with far more speed than any normal fuel. All without being consumed in the process. It was, as far as Wugong could tell, one step short of a perpetual motion device. The only caveat was that it was temperamental; quite literally possessing a mind of its own, and required constant encouragement. They'd been able to provide that with electrical impulses but only for short periods.

Yet again Wugong regretted the loss of his bracelet and cursed the foreign devil woman who'd stolen it. The bracelet was the most important part of the living metal, containing the consciousness that controlled the rest. Without it, the stuff in the jar was only capable of the most rudimentary emotions, most of which were anger and obstinacy. He had to get it back, even if he had to break every bone in that woman's body to do so. Or, better yet, he'd get it off her by the simple expedient of cutting her arm off with it.

"I'm becoming a laughingstock," Soong growled, glaring at Wugong. "And your failures are not helping. Between them and that damned dragon burning down our hideout, it's looking like I can't keep my organization in line."

Fortunately for Wugong, a street kid came to the door right then. Not only did that distract Soong from his grim focus on their failures but it made the boy, a huge, almost ox-like youth whose big and obviously empty head brushed the top of the doorway, the object of Soong's ire. "Well?" Soong demanded when the kid stopped and stared wildly at him, obviously realizing he'd walked into the ogre's den without so much as a sacrificial offering; a failure that could easily make him the ogre's dinner instead. "What is it?"

"They said you wanted to know where that GI Joe was taken and who took him."

"Well? Don't stand there drooling at me," Soong snapped. "Talk!"

"Zhao Zhu had him. He was just dumped in front of the American Consulate by one of Zhao's men."

That wasn't good. Zhao Zhu was one of the Soong gang's rivals, as well as being one of Pockmarked Wong's enemies. He was rumored to have ties with the communists and his house, an old castle atop *Chinglung* Mountain near West Lake, was said to be a maze of traps. If the jar were in his treasury, it would be one hell of a job getting the damned thing back.

A thought occurred to Wugong and he coughed. "Soong, there's one man who could break into Zhao's and get the jar without problems." For a moment Soong seemed puzzled, then he smiled approvingly as he took Wugong's meaning. Chen Tang had been hanging around the gang for days now and doing sweet nothing at all. Given he was said to be so good he could have stolen the royal seal off the Emperor's Chief Eunuch, had such a thing still existed, he was the most obvious choice.

"Yes," Soong said. "An excellent thought. Go find him. It's high time that annoying little sneak made himself useful."

⟨⟨⟨

Chapter Twelve
Nightlife in Shanghai Begins With the Tea-Cocktail Hour

The Hunt was over and done by the time they returned. Not, Conall realized, because the hunters had finished but because the dragon's appearance had spooked everyone's horses so badly that the only one who'd not fallen off was that fellow Mudan called the Black Jade Fox. He was sitting on his mount grinning broadly at the confusion, to everyone else's obvious annoyance.

It surprised Conall that no one had noticed that he and his companions had been missing throughout the excitement. Instead, two hours after the event, the hunters were still exclaiming loudly over how terrible an insult the whole thing was. Only a few seemed actually worried about those riders who hadn't returned yet.

"Where the devil is Sir Bruce?" Murtagh demanded as he handed his reins to a stable-boy and stripped his mud covered coat off. "And who was that fool up there flying around like a maniac? Bad enough he startled all the horses, diving on us like that. He could have set fire to the field with his flame throwers!"

Conall almost asked what fool Murtagh meant before he realized the man thought the dragon had been a plane. Had the dragon created an illusion to keep outsiders from seeing him? Or was it because most people, faced with a thing so completely outside expectation like a dragon, ignored what they saw in favor of what they believed it ought to be? Either was possible, especially with a man like Murtagh.

One thing suggested the latter. When the Hunt had started there'd been several dozen farmers watching the festivities and shouting angry, impotent, insults. Conall had guessed from their behavior that they'd have loved to see the entire Paper Chase Hunt Club going arse over teakettle. Instead of staying to point and laugh, they'd all disappeared from sight.

When Conall asked Murtagh what had happened to the farmers it took the man a moment to understand. "Those nuisances? Don't worry about them. They took it into their heads that we were being attacked and ran for it."

"They were shouting something about tea, I think. At least, I heard oolong in there," Striker offered uncertainly as he joined them.

Somewhere behind Conall, Zhanchi made a noise between a snort and a snarl. Fortunately, for his continued employment, he kept his mouth shut, though it was obviously a challenge for him. Quickly, to keep Zhanchi out of trouble, Conall asked. "Oolong means black dragon, doesn't it, Mudan?"

"Yes." she agreed serenely. "This may not be the first time that flyer has caused trouble. Perhaps that is the nickname they have given it. Certainly it looked nothing like a proper dragon to me." That last was said in a pointed way and Conall knew she'd aimed her words directly at him. He smiled, knowing her bite to be as bad or worse than her bark, yet fearing neither. No matter how irritating he might be to her, she would never harm him. It was confidence some said he ought not have, yet he couldn't help but be sure of it.

Striker looked around. "I wouldn't know," he admitted. "But for now, isn't it high time we got to work? I realize we want everyone to think we're on vacation, but that doesn't mean we have to fiddle around for days before getting the job done."

"First we have to convince Mr. Soong to permit McLeod to look at the engine," Murtagh pointed out. "And Sir Bruce is the only one Mr. Soong is willing to talk to."

Even Conall thought that only made a fishy situation smell even fishier. He could understand not wanting to risk having one's invention stolen, but if this Mr. Soong couldn't provide proof that it worked at all, there was a good chance it didn't do more than look and sound pretty.

Striker had described the one demonstration of the engine to Conall before and everything about what he'd said had suggested how easy it would be to trick the viewers. The demonstration had been performed on the ground, with the engine set on a large covered table. Cables and wires had gone everywhere, or so it'd seemed to Striker. Hiding a second engine, even a third, to create the force needed to turn the propeller so fast would have been simple. Nor would it be the first time such a trick had been played on hopeful investors.

"And I've just received word that Mr. Soong has promised to meet me at the Eastern Star this evening." Sir Bruce came striding up, looking as if he'd been through the wringer. When everyone exclaimed at the sight of him, he added, "Don't you worry, now. Just took a bit of a tumble in a creek. Spent some time looking for the rats that tripped me in and had to dry off."

"I wish you'd stop disappearing all the time," Murtagh grumbled. "And what do you mean, the Eastern Star?"

"A cabaret. They hired a singer, Manuela, to perform tonight and I understand she's considered beyond talented." Sir Bruce shrugged. "Couldn't say, myself. Got a tin ear."

Striker sighed, "Well, if it gets us a look at that plane engine, I'm all for it. What time?"

"With my cook gone missing—bad joss to her and all her kin—we'll have to eat at the Evening Star," Sir Bruce told him, gesturing in the general direction of his house. "We'll have to dress for dinner. Hope you've all brought something appropriate to wear. Wouldn't want to look like something the cat dragged in, now would we?"

((((

The Eastern Star was one of Shanghai's many, many, nightclubs. So many that, according to Conall, his guidebook's author had apparently waxed eloquent over their existence until he'd sounded like an over-excited child going to the candy store. "Dog races and cabarets, hai-alai and cabarets, formal tea and dinner dances and cabarets…," he read aloud to Mudan and Striker as Shen drove them through the brightly lit and colorful streets of the city. "Whoopee!"

Mudan watched Conall talk and had to work to keep her expression straight. His bright red hair was wildly disarrayed and his bow tie was off at an angle that made her yearn to fix it back in place. As for his dinner jacket, he'd somehow managed to button it askew. Honestly, she didn't know what to do with him, sometimes. "I did not know you enjoyed such things."

"I don't," Conall admitted. "But this fellow did." He held up the book and from up front, Shen murmured something derogatory in a form of Chinese Mudan barely understood. "Don't scoff, Shen. I'm sure it'll be invaluable to someone, someday."

Striker laughed. "Perhaps, but that book's not important. I didn't want to mention how long you were gone in front of Sir Bruce, but I did notice. Noticed you had that driver of Murtagh's with you when you came back. How'd that come about?"

"He was bored, so we let him tag along," Conall explained. "Can hardly blame him. He's a pilot, not a chauffer. Until that engine is ready to test, he's grounded."

"I see." Striker shook his head. "Just like Murtagh to waste that poor kid's time making him drive him hither and yon. No wonder he always looks so grim. But whatever took you so long?"

"We ran into a fight with the same man who attacked us before. According to Zhanchi, his name is Feng Wugong." Mudan decided not to reveal the two men's relationship; she was now quite sure Zhanchi had nothing to do with his brother. "He and his men were following a group of American soldiers, rather than ourselves. He got away, but the police were quite annoyed with us for our involvement."

"Can't really blame them," Conall said. "Tourists aren't supposed to join in street fights. But those were our fellow citizens Woogang attacked." At her raised brow, he adjusted his pronunciation and tried again. "Wugong?"

"Better," Mudan agreed. "It is not your fault. You did not grow up hearing the words every day."

Again Striker interrupted. "I won't scold you for getting involved. I can tell it would go in one ear and out the other. But do you have an idea of what this fellow Wuhgoon was up to?"

Not bothering to correct Striker's pronunciation, despite the way Shen flinched, Mudan said, "Whatever it was, he did not deign to inform me." She wouldn't mention the jar. That, and the bracelet she wore, surely had nothing to do with Striker's business. "He left quickly, at the command of one of the others with him. A man he called Soong."

"That's the name of the fellow selling us the engine," Striker said thoughtfully. "Now I'm sure something's up."

Quite suddenly, and without embarrassment for eavesdropping, Shen said, "Soong is the boss of a gang associated with Pockmarked Huang."

Striker opened his mouth to complain about Shen's interruption; according to his lights a driver ought not pay attention to their boss's business. Before he could, Mudan put a hand on his wrist to stop him. "Shen knows the city better than I, Mr. Striker. And he assisted us in the fight. I think he can be trusted."

Doubtfully, Striker answered, "Well, if you say so, Mudan. You're your father's daughter and Chang is a savvy old bird."

"I believe it would please him to know you think that," Mudan answered, although she'd prefer not to think too hard on her father at all. As long as she didn't, she needn't acknowledge to herself just how unhappy he was going to be over where she was and what she was up to. The days when the Jeen Loon decapitated disobedient crewmembers were long past, but there were still ways for its leader to punish an unruly daughter. Not least being the fact that she hated making him sad.

Fortunately, Chang was far away in Strikersport and with luck it would be some time before he found out where she was. Hopefully before then she'd work out a way to tell him. Convincing him to let her marry Conall, however, might still be beyond her powers.

"We're here," Shen said suddenly, drawing to a halt behind another limo. Murtagh's, Mudan realized and once the man had climbed out and turned to wait for him, saw his driver flutter his fingers at them insouciantly. Murtagh growled angrily at Zhanchi, who immediately snapped to attention and drove the car away. "I will go keep that impulsive youngster company. If fortune is with us, we won't run into trouble."

Not said, but implied by Shen's tone was the man's suspicion that Mudan, Conall and Striker would not be so lucky.

⟨⟨⟨

Zhanchi sat back and sulked. It wasn't being scolded that annoyed him so much as the fact that he wanted, desperately, to do something, anything, that wasn't sitting in a driver's seat waiting. He couldn't be sure, among the city's lights, but he thought the sky was clear and cool, the very place he'd rather be. Flying at night wasn't easy, but it was a challenge he enjoyed. The moon would be full soon and he could imagine it shining on the landscape below, gleaming off fields, its reflection glittering in the water.

A tap on his window made Zhanchi look out to find Shen standing beside the car. Apparently the other driver was as bored as he and wanted company. Well, if that was the case, Zhanchi was his man. They couldn't discuss that dragon or anything else about their day, for fear of being overheard, but there was far more to Shen then just a driver. With luck, Zhanchi might figure out what.

"Lock your car and come with me," Shen ordered once Zhanchi had joined him.

"Come with you?" Zhanchi obeyed and trailed behind Shen to a darker alley. Most of this area was brightly lit, courtesy of the sheer number of nightclubs, bars and dives, but there were always places one could lurk, if lurking was required.

A thought occurred to Zhanchi. "I'm not that sort," he said as they stepped into the shadows. "If that's what you're looking for." His voice trailed off as it occurred to him that if he were wrong he'd just been horribly offensive.

"What I require is a little more obscure," Shen said. "And at the moment, hardly important to our mission."

"Our mission?" Zhanchi repeated.

"It wasn't yours to start with, I admit, but here you are, deeply entangled in a thing I must do. And it will surely be better than sitting in a car awaiting a purblind fool's pleasure."

Plaintively, because all Zhanchi wanted out of life was a plane and a sky to fly it in, he protested, "I'm only involved on the side. And can't you get that Bai She fellow to help you? He's obviously a powerful sorcerer." So was Shen, it occurred to Zhanchi belatedly, uncertain how he knew.

Grimly, Shen said, "Bai She is far from his place and his strength depends entirely on what little faith he can garner in this land. Your brother injured him badly and he has not yet recovered." The man eyed Zhanchi critically. "I am not asking for sorcery from you. I can, as you surmise, provide that. But your assistance will be needed. You may even be called upon to fly... yes, I thought that would get your attention."

"If you can get me flying, Shen, I will worship you forever." The words were out of Zhanchi's mouth before he could stop them.

"Not forever, Zhanchi. No mortal lasts that long." Shen chuckled at the expression on Zhanchi's face. "Now then, I must protect Mudan until she has completed the task her God gave her. That means, in turn, I must protect McLeod."

That would prove difficult right now. Those two were inside the Eastern Star, a place where gangsters, lords and businessmen mixed regularly. Any of McLeod, or Mudan's, enemies could be there, preparing to harm them. However, "We're just drivers, you realize. They won't let us in."

"Not if they don't know we're drivers," Shen pointed out and before Zhanchi could counter that they couldn't help looking the part in their chauffer uniforms and hats, the man snapped his fingers. His clothing changed, becoming fine dark purple-tinted silk and linen. The lines of the suit were perfect and even Zhanchi could tell it had the sort of quality that required a personal tailor and far more money than sense to possess.

It took Zhanchi a moment to realize that his own clothing had changed, or appeared to have changed as well, and to something very similar. "McLeod will see right through this," he pointed out, remembering the American's peculiar talent.

"McLeod may appear to have no brain inside his head but he is not the fool he pretends to be. If he sees and recognizes us, he will not speak," Shen answered. "Now. Come along. We have work to do and we've already wasted more time than I like."

Chapter Thirteen
There's Nothing Puritanical About Shanghai

Wugong watched the Eastern Star's main room fill with a mix of satisfaction and worry. He was glad to see the number of customers who'd come to listen to Manuela sing. Was glad to see the alcohol pouring out of bottles and into people at very nearly the same rate. Was glad to see the money leaving one set of hands to make its home in his safe. He was even glad to see that Sir Bruce had—as hoped—persuaded his guests to join him at the nightclub. What worried him, though, was how to get McLeod away from the rest so they could capture him.

It didn't help that the man in question only seemed interested in talking to either Striker or Striker's mistress. He watched the dancing, listened to the music and quietly and slowly sipped at his drink in a way that suggested that there were hundreds of places he'd rather be. Not even the obvious charms of Lord William's companion, a pretty little Japanese girl dressed in an elegant Western style gown of light blue chiffon and silk, seemed to register on him. Was it Wugong's imagination, or was the girl actually flirting with McLeod right there in front of her patron?

Poor form if that were true. At least that girl of Striker's had the sense not to make her interest in the engineer obvious. She was ignoring McLeod almost entirely, answering him without bothering to look in his direction. She barely seemed to notice his frequent compliments of her appearance. Wugong had to admit she'd outdone herself, her dark hair carefully coiffured and pinned by peonies and an old-fashioned red and gold satin robe embroidered with dragons and more peonies. It almost made him wonder if she really were Chinese after all.

As for Lord William, he was apparently turning his interest on Striker's mistress, offering her drinks, plying her with food and generally making a nuisance of himself. Perhaps that was why the Japanese girl felt it safe to play? Not that any of this mattered. He needed to get McLeod alone and quickly.

Wugong didn't dare approach the group but he moved so he was in just the right position to hear them talk about inconsequential matters. Sir Bruce and Lord William were talking about the Paper Chase Hunt; McLeod was flipping through a guide book and reading it aloud. The Japanese girl was commenting vivaciously and hinting that she wanted to dance. Through it all, Striker's woman kept silent, although her eye twitched occasionally as if she were irritated. Good, Wugong thought. Let her be.

Considering his options, Wugong was about to try having one of the waiters pour a tray of champagne on McLeod's head. The manager would then draw the young man away from his party to see to the damage to his suit, giving them a chance to take him.

Before he could do anything of the sort, however, the Japanese girl did it for him, spilling half her glass of red wine down the man's shirt. "Oh. Oh my God, I am so sorry!" she fussed. "Here. Let me help you. I'll get some water and clean it up!"

McLeod stopped her and stood up. "I'll go wash it off," he said. "I won't be long."

Well enough, Wugong thought. This wasn't what he'd intended, but it'd had the desired effect. The foreign devil woman couldn't follow McLeod into the men's room, and Wugong could. Or, even better, he could be there first. He headed towards the washroom, intending to take advantage of the first moment he could to grab his target.

Wugong reached the hall to the washroom before McLeod. He knew the back halls of the nightclub well and figured it'd be easier to get the man this way. He wouldn't even need his men for this. All he needed was one centipede at the right time. Or maybe two. McLeod was skinny but he was tall.

Listening from behind the door, Wugong soon heard footsteps that sounded like a clumsy young calf stumbling to its mother. Having watched McLeod walk, he was fairly sure that was him. To his surprise, though, the footsteps stopped a dozen or so feet away.

Not daring to peek out, in case his target saw and recognized him, Wugong listened and sighed. He should have expected this, he thought, as Lord William's wench said, "You must feel sad to be all alone out here. Your employer has a woman. You should have a woman."

That made Wugong crack the door to the washroom just enough to see McLeod leaning against the wall, staring down at the much smaller girl with wide and startled eyes. A moment later Wugong closed the door quickly and hoped he hadn't been seen. Trouble was coming of the sort he wanted no part of. Striker's woman was headed towards the other two and her emotionless expression was chilling. He almost felt sorry for the Japanese girl.

((((

Mudan ignored Wugong's attempt to hide in the washroom. As long as Conall stayed where he was the man couldn't act without revealing himself. Whereas Fukushima was already a risk. "Get away from him. Now," she said, as calmly as she could considering how very nearly she'd failed Conall.

"Obasan, you obviously have a man already. Why be greedy?"

The insult made both Mudan's brows go up and she stared at Fukushima for a moment. "Obasan?" she repeated. "My Japanese is not strong, I admit, but don't you think grandmother is overdoing it a bit?"

"Old lady, you just don't have enough of what it takes," Fukushima answered, obviously trying to anger Mudan into striking first. She very nearly got what she wanted, pushed up against Conall the way she was. Conall's panicked expression alone was enough to infuriate her into action. If Mudan weren't absolutely certain Fukushima was pretending to seduce him, she would have demonstrated the famed temper of the Jeen Loon's Fire Dragon without hesitation.

Instead, more to test her theory than to actually injure, Mudan stepped in and used an eagle claw strike. As expected, Fukushima jerked backwards and instinctively blocked. Then, realizing she'd revealed more than she'd meant to, she stumbled back and cried out like a little child. "Don't hurt me."

"Nonsense," Mudan said. "Leave Conall alone and go away and I won't have to do a single thing."

"I am not leaving." The foot stomp Fukushima gave was a nearly perfect imitation of a spoiled brat but it was too studied to be real. "You go."

"No. Where Conall goes, I go."

"You'll get yourself dismissed! Your master won't put up with you chasing after another man!"

Mudan eyed the woman thoughtfully, trying to decide whose side she was on. The only way to find out would be to ask. As Conall protested, she moved, catching hold of Fukushima's arm and pulling her close. "Listen and do not interrupt," she hissed. "If you're here to help Wugong abduct Conall, I promise you, I'll break your neck first."

Real surprise flared in Fukushima's eyes. "Wugong? Feng Wugong?" Her tone deepened as she spoke and her posture shifted from annoying brat child to that of a soldier. "What does he have to do with this?"

"The Soong gang wants Conall and Wugong is waiting in that washroom for him."

Before Mudan could say another word, Wugong stepped out and this time he wasn't bothering with magic. Now that he knew Mudan could counter his centipedes, he'd gone to the time-honored tradition of gangsters everywhere and drawn his gun.

Mudan sighed, gazing at the man with rising exasperation. "You are becoming quite the thorn in my side," she said quietly, dropping her hands and stepping between him and Conall. The gun centered itself on her and she went still, hoping Conall wouldn't take it into his head to play the hero.

That was a vain hope. After all the attempts on him, from centipedes to poison to gunplay, and with Mudan at risk to protect him, Conall was at the end of his patience. Now it was he stepping between her and Wugong, putting himself close enough the man could have grabbed him any time. "No more," he said grimly.

Fukushima took advantage of Wugong's distraction to fling a dagger at him. If Conall hadn't been partly in her way she might have gotten the gangster in the throat. With Conall there, though, the best she could do was bury it in Wugong's shoulder. It was almost enough to make him drop his gun but not quite.

"No more indeed," Wugong snapped, speaking in English. "The two of you back off. McLeod, you're the one I want. Come here."

Despairingly, Mudan could tell Conall would have handed himself over without a fight. Then hope flared as her bracelet shifted around her wrist. Without looking at it, she made a slight motion towards Wugong. She hoped it understood, for she dared not open her mouth to speak.

It acted quickly, releasing its hold on her arm and running down her silk skirt, snagging the embroidery as it passed. Before Wugong could react, it swarmed up inside his trouser leg, setting him dancing as he pounded at the thing crawling its way towards all too sensitive parts. The lump beneath his clothes moved steadily despite his efforts and finally burst out from near the top of his shirt, where it reared up and bit Wugong on the nose.

Shots fired; an alarming consequence to Wugong's attempt to get rid of his attacker. Mudan grabbed both Fukushima and Conall and dragged them back, rushing them towards the main dining room. This wasn't the time for heroics. This was the time for escape.

The sound of a strangely familiar drumbeat and chimes made Mudan slow to a halt as they stepped out into the room. A small troupe of Chinese actors were gathered on the dance floor, led by a very tall man dressed in dark blue silk finery. Although his face was hidden behind a form-fitting mask, Mudan recognized his clean-cut features immediately. The Faithful Hound of Fragrant Mountain.

As Wugong flung himself at them, she sidestepped, tripping him automatically, eyes still on the newcomer as he spread his arms and announced, "Ladies and Gentlemen, allow me to introduce myself. I am the Master of Ceremonies of this band of merry revelers. We come to you at great expense from the Fragrant Stone Theater to bring you one of our finest shows. The Dance of the Golden Dragon!"

《《《

Conall stared raptly, admiring the chaos one small group of acrobats could achieve. Dozens of young men and women in elaborate costumes covered with embroidery rushed about the room. They carried mounds of yellow silk that they were tossing out to the crowd. One carried a dragon head so like the one he'd seen used back in Strikersport that it could have been its twin. Its wielder was snapping its jaws and flinging himself about wildly as he waited for the others to prepare themselves.

"The dragon gains strength with every participant," the ringleader announced. "We invite you to join in, to make the dragon grow." Behind him, the band began to play a rousing tune that set all the performers leaping and twisting around as they caught hold of the guests and drew them in to join them. Even Manuela joined the fun, dancing on stage and teasing the holder of the dragon head with little flirting motions.

Wugong was cursing somewhere to the side but Conall could see he was no longer armed. Or, rather, his gun was no longer useful, having been bitten in half by the little silver dragon. The creature rushed back to Mudan and climbed up on her shoulder to sit there like a cat. It belched contentedly, a little puff of sulfur scented smoke trailing from its open mouth.

"Manners, Child of Dream," Mudan said. "Conall, Miss Fukushima, we should get out of here. Now."

Spotting a familiar, if unexpected, figure beckoning to him from the other side of the room, Conall said, "There's Shen. And Zhanchi." He wondered how the pair had gotten in dressed like drivers but decided not to ask. Just in case this was another illusion and one he shouldn't reveal.

"Then we shall go to him." They slipped past the crowd, growing loud and unruly with the excitement of the dance that was now wending its way through the dining area, knocking over chairs as it went. Miss Fukushima was behind them and while he was sure she was one of the ones wanting to capture him, he was also sure she wasn't with Wugong.

"It seems we were not necessary after all," Shen said as soon as they reached him.

"We're not out of the woods yet," Conall answered, pointing at the men dressed as waiters headed their way. They didn't look happy and the pistols they carried only made things worse. "Can that pet of yours eat all their guns, Mudan?"

"No need," Zhanchi said, pointing. The crowd of dancers were excitedly leaping and twisting towards them and the waiters put their weapons away. At a guess, they weren't ready to risk official attention by accidentally shooting the wrong person.

The dragon dance swirled around Mudan and Conall and their ringmaster leaned down to whisper in her ear. Whatever he said, it obviously worried her. Then the dance was gone again, having swept the waiters in its wake; leaving a clear path for the door.

They ran for it immediately and when they reached it, Shen said, "Zhanchi will lead you to the car. I'll keep the others from following."

As Zhanchi did as Shen ordered, Conall snuck a look behind him and saw Shen standing in the doorway blocking Wugong's men. They were trying again, he saw, and held his breath a moment. Then electricity flared around the driver, forming a wall that kept their pursuit from following. Shen turned and raised a brow at Conall, just as Mudan came back to grab him by the elbow and drag him along. "This is not the time," she grumbled at him when he tried to work out what Shen had done.

Within a few minutes they were down the street to where Zhanchi and Shen had parked. "I remember saying to follow Zhanchi," Shen said as he settled into his car.

"You must forgive him," Mudan answered as she forced Conall into the back seat. "His curiosity far outweighs his sense."

Conall couldn't argue the point, so he didn't. Instead he slid in further, so Miss Fukushima could join them. She was too deeply involved to leave behind. At the same time Shen started his car and gestured for Zhanchi to get in beside him. When Zhanchi hesitated, Shen ordered, "You want to fly, right? You won't with him. Not until you've proved yourself."

That made Zhanchi's mind up for him and he climbed in. They were just barely in time. Behind them, a half dozen other cars were headed their way. They were fast but Shen was faster, his car purring silently through the streets of Shanghai. "Where do we go?" he asked finally, once it was clear he'd lost their pursuit before it had managed to find them.

"I was told we would be safe at Fragrant Stone theater," Mudan said, sounding unsure of herself.

"But can we trust them? Just because they showed up in time to save us, that doesn't make them our allies," Miss Fukushima argued.

"They may not be yours," Mudan said with a smile that held very little humor. "But they are mine. Fragrant Stone Theater is one of my father's many holdings and its actors all belong to the Jeen Loon."

Chapter Fourteen
Chinese Theater is Another Institution of Interest

"You might at least pretend to be enjoying yourself."

Kurumata looked sideways at his commander and did his level best not to snarl his answer. "This is nonsense." He gestured towards the stage below them, where Chinese acrobats were leaping back and forth in an admittedly splendid display of cooperation and athleticism. Dressed in foolish costumes, singing in high-pitched voices and accompanied by sounds they no doubt believed to be musical, to Kurumata it was just another demonstration of Shanghai's decadent nature. Why, they even had a woman playing a woman's role, a thing unheard of in Japan.

Slowly, he said, "I don't understand why we're here." He was desperately uncomfortable in Western evening wear and wanted nothing more than a yukata and quiet room.

"Listen to all the noise, Kurumata," Shikawa said, as if that were an answer. "You can hardly hear yourself think."

Kurumata shrugged. "And?"

"And that means no one but those close to us can hear either. And

" THAT MADE ZANCHI'S
MIND UP FOR HIM AND HE
CLIMBED IN. "

since we have a private box, we can speak without risking being overheard. We are, after all, just watching the Fragrant Stone Theater's excellent performance in comfort." Shikawa gestured around them, indicating the elegant red and gold decorated chamber that overlooked the stage from above the rest of the audience.

The room was one of several, each set so one couldn't look into any of the others. It was also chilly and dim and Kurumata kept having the oddest feeling of being watched even though he'd checked for spies several times. Ignoring his Lieutenant's discomfort, Shikawa added, "It is the perfect place to meet our informant."

That person had yet to arrive, although the show was now almost half over and Kurumata was certain the bastard wasn't coming. Fortunately, he didn't make a fool of himself by saying so, because just as he thought that, the door behind them opened and a voluptuous Chinese woman entered. Dressed in a dark blue cheongsam of velvet, with fur trim and silk embroidery, Kurumata recognized her immediately as his former prisoner.

"Zhi Lin, you've met my Lieutenant, Kurumata. Kurumata, the young lady has news for us regarding the item we're looking for. Don't you, Zhi Lin?"

The woman inclined her head and sat down beside Shikawa. "I've been sent by my master to speak with you about the device."

Both Shikawa and Kurumata straightened. "Your... master?" Kurumata demanded. He'd thought Zhi Lin was a freelancer, accepting employment from whoever could pay enough. "You have a master?"

"I was trained by Warlord Zhao. Ordinarily, he allows me the freedom to act on my own. But once he learned about the device, and realized how many were interested in it, he commanded me to become involved." Zhi Lin spread her hands, as if to ask, 'what can one do?'

"Which means Zhao is now yet another of the many players hunting the device," Shikawa sighed, acknowledging the news with barely a frown. Then he stood up and applauded as the acrobats finished their routine and bowed. "Quite good," he pronounced. "Some of the best I've seen in Shanghai."

As the scene changed, revealing the next scene in a story Kurumata had been barely following; a pale haired actor stepped on stage and began to play a silver flute. For once it was a man playing a woman's part, as it should be. Madam White Snake, seducing her scholarly lover and defied by the Buddhist monk convinced she was an evil demon. Kurumata neither knew, nor cared, why.

Zhi Lin waited until the scholar began singing before saying, "Master Zhao is not hunting the device," she told Shikawa. "Because he has captured it."

They both turned to look at her and it was Shikawa who said, in a voice almost loud enough to be heard over the performance, "What!" Realizing his mistake, he said more quietly. "How the hell did he get it?"

Reflecting he seldom saw his superior flustered, Kurumata asked quietly, "If Zhao has it and you are here to tell us at his behest, I assume he wishes to bargain." No way such a man would give his prize freely.

"I hesitate to guess at my master's plans, Lieutenant. All I know is that he commands a meeting. He suggests the Willow Pattern Tea House in the Old City, at noon tomorrow. He will not attend himself, of course, but once everyone has arrived, I will present his suggestions." Zhi Lin rose. "Do you agree?"

Kurumata didn't like this at all. He didn't pay a great deal of attention to the Chinese gangs, except when they got in his way, but Zhao was—by all reports—a dangerous and tricky devil. "It's a trap."

"It is not," Zhi Lin denied. "Although he told me to tell you he understands that you would think so. It is for that reason he suggests the tea house. It is a public place and you and the others invited will have plenty of time to make sure no one waits to harm you. As well as to ensure you are not recognized, if that is your desire."

Grimly, Shikawa said, "Kurumata will be there. Tell your master if the Lieutenant does not return, unharmed, we have a simple way to deal with the issue. One that will not require any of my men risk the dangers of his legendary traps. The device he holds is not so important that we won't bomb his mansion out of existence should it become necessary. Better no one have it, than it fall into the wrong hands."

"My master expected you would say such a thing," Zhi Lin replied smoothly. "He wishes me to tell you he understands, entirely, the need to bluster and boast. I will meet you tomorrow, as planned."

As Zhi Lin slipped out of the box, Shikawa looked at Kurumata. "Follow her," he ordered.

It was a thing easier to command than to obey, Kurumata thought as he left the box. The woman wasn't stupid enough to think she wouldn't be followed. Nor was Kurumata trained in the art of stealth, being a soldier first and foremost. Still, he trailed behind Zhi Lin, keeping as close as he dared. She was going downstairs and he could at least claim to be headed for the lavatory if she noticed him.

If she did see him, it didn't matter. Once she'd reached to first floor of the theater she walked straight across to the stairs on the other side of the lobby, where two Chinese men stood watch. They were an odd pair, one quite tall and lean, with a thick brush of black hair and an overly serious expression, the other slightly shorter, with an irrepressibly cheeky grin. He looked rather like he'd been teasing his fellow just as Zhi Lin approached.

Kurumata paused to watch from a safe distance. Once his quarry had spoken to the pair and gone past, he attempted to follow suit, only to find the smaller man's arm barring his way. Smirking, the fellow shook his head. "Sorry. Private box."

"I'm with the woman," Kurumata tried, knowing it was nonsense. No one would believe a man like himself would chase a woman that way.

"Yeah? Well you can wait for her here, then. The owner wants privacy." His companion glared at him. "What?"

"Your mouth's too big. Don't talk about the Boss's business."

Kurumata could tell that the only way he was getting past was by making a scene. Shikawa wouldn't want that. "Never mind. I'll look for her later. It's a surprise, though, so don't tell her I was here."

"Sure. Whatever you want."

As Kurumata headed back to rejoin his boss he was almost certain the one man was making horrible faces at him from behind his back. Under most circumstances he'd teach the insolent wretch a lesson, but that would draw far too much attention.

He'd reached the stairs when he noticed a small group entering the theater. An American, by his walk and speech, two Chinese men, one Chinese woman and, lastly and disconcertingly, Fukushima. Now what was she up to? And why was that one Chinese man oddly familiar?

⟨⟨⟨

Zhi Lin didn't have to go far to find her master. He'd taken a box on the other side of the theater and all she had to do was go down some steps, get past the theater's security and up some others to reach it. An inconvenience, those two, but at least they stopped that idiot Japanese who'd tried to follow her.

Those two keeping watch also warned her to expect company. They certainly weren't there to keep an eye on Master Zhao. He'd come to the theater in his usual disguise as a local businessman and it would look strange for him to have any companion except his First Wife. That worthy would be in the theater box with him, using her spells to protect him from any and all who might try to attack.

Thus Zhi Lin was unsurprised to find another man sitting with her master. He cut a strange figure compared to the conservative business suit Master Zhao wore. Indeed, everything about him seemed direct contrast to the Warlord. Thin as Zhao was thick, the man was dressed in a yellow robe worthy of the exiled Emperor of China. His face was concealed behind a dragon painted mask so perfectly fit to his features that it seemed to move with his expression. He was dressed in an embroidered yellow robe that would have gotten him executed for treason less than a century earlier and a feathered hat that covered his steel grey hair. At Zhi Lin's entrance he smiled dourly.

"There you are, Zhi Lin. Did the Japanese give you any trouble?" At her hesitation, her master added, with a snaggletoothed grin, "Oh, Master Dragon isn't one of the players in this game. He's our host, the mysterious owner of the Fragrant Stone Theater. It is rare indeed for him to make an appearance. He honors us with his presence." Now Zhi Lin understood the outfit. No one had ever seen Master Dragon without it, a peculiar conceit that most regarded as an actor's love of drama.

"Oh no, it is we who are honored, Mr. Tsao," the stranger said smoothly. "It is rare that you condescend to visit any theater. That you choose ours is an unexpected pleasure. I could not help but thank you for your attention."

Below, Madam White Snake was singing a beautiful rendition of the character's lament. Trapped and bound for eternity by the monk, she would never see her lover again. The scholar sang in turn, promising to wait for her for as long as the moon shone and the rivers flowed. It was one of the most beautiful and moving moments in the play and—as always—Zhi Lin yearned to slap both the scholar and his lover as hard as she could. What did they know about love, about sacrifice, or filial piety?

"Your new performer is excellent," Master Zhao said as the song ended.

"He is. But he doesn't get along well with the others. I doubt he'll be staying long." The man calling himself Dragon shrugged. "Still, he's been quite useful."

Zhi Lin eyed the man playing Madam White Snake thoughtfully. Beneath the stage make-up, his features had an arrogant cast that suggested he didn't get along well with many people. She didn't say so, however, knowing her input was neither desired nor necessary. Instead she waited behind Master Zhao, feeling a sharp chill. Best not mention it in it front of the theater's owner. It would be discourteous to complain that every one of his theater boxes had one hell of a draft.

After a few more words, Master Dragon had left the box. Zhi Lin breathed a sigh of relief. She'd been worried he might ask her questions that she mustn't answer. Worse, he was the sort to see through any sort of attempt to dissemble. His black eyes were sharp and knowing behind his mask.

Master Zhao waited a moment before asking, "We are private?"

"Nothing breathes here but us," his wife said, bowing her head. "I would know it."

"Then report, daughter. Tell me what I need to know."

Zhi Lin bowed. "As my brother will have told you, he successfully warned Soong that you have the device I stole for you. Soong is sending a thief called Chen Tang to try and steal it back."

"I see. One of the few men who might, perhaps, have a chance to get past my traps. Though I think it likely that the Black Jade Fox will have stuck his sharp and curious nose too deeply, should he make the attempt." Master Zhao smiled. "And what of your visit to Shikawa?"

"I invited him to the tea house tomorrow as you ordered. He threatened violence to the castle should any harm come to his agent, but did not refuse."

"Good. Then all that remains is to enjoy this lovely play before returning home for a good night's rest. Tomorrow shall be a very busy day indeed, daughter, and I expect you to be ready to play your part."

Zhi Lin bowed. "Father, I am your most dutiful and obedient child. Anything you ask of me, I will do."

⟪⟪⟪

There were few things that pleased Grant-Merchant as much as inconveniencing someone he disliked. Inconveniencing someone who'd interfered with military business and pulled strings to get his little desires fulfilled only made it sweeter. No one, he felt, could blame him for keeping an eye on Miss Fukushima after Lord William had left with her. No one could blame him for being in the right place at the right time to see the girl cause trouble for an American chap and fight with a Chinese girl. No one could blame him for following her after gangsters at the nightclub tried to do her and the others harm. And no one could possibly blame him for deciding she was up to something and bringing her in for questioning. Again.

Watching Miss Fukushima, together with the American and—now—

three Chinese enter the Fragrant Stone Theater, he promised himself he'd get proper answers from her or he'd know the reason why. He followed them into the building and immediately found an unexpected and familiar face. Joe Croydon was an old friend, for they used the same club and frequented the same establishments. He knew the officer well enough to be sure he wouldn't willingly attend a Chinese play. Anymore, it occurred to Grant-Merchant, than he, himself would.

The two of them looked at each other uncertainly. "Well this is a coincidence," Grant-Merchant said, hoping to make light of his presence. He couldn't tell Croydon what was up; that engine of Soong's was military business. Yet at the same time he had no idea how to explain his presence that didn't make him sound like a fool.

Before Croydon could answer, the ticket seller closed the shade to his booth, causing both men to turn on him. "Hey," Croydon said. "The show isn't over until midnight!" He looked at Grant-Merchant, adding quietly, "There's some suspicious chappies I've been trying to keep an eye on. They ran out of the Eastern Star a little while ago and I've been following them ever since."

The ticket-seller paused as he headed for what was obviously a staff entrance. "No can do tickee. Is full."

"Now youee waitee here. Am poleese. You lettee them other peeples in."

It was the very worst example of pidgin-English Grant-Merchant had ever heard, a reminder that Croydon hated everything about Shanghai, up to and including trying to talk to the Chinese. Quickly, so as not to cause a fight, he asked the ticket-seller. "You understand English?"

"Maybe so."

"You tell why we not go in?"

"Full house. Last tickee sold."

Croydon grumbled. "The hell. It's not like they don't just crowd in. Can't count the number of times I've found this kind of place packed like a tin of sardines!"

"Full up here," the ticket seller said firmly, tapping his chin to make the point. "No room. No way."

With a curse, Croydon turned around. "I'm going to see what I can do about getting some persuasion. Do me a favor. Wait here and watch for a group of four Chinese with an American. Fellow's about so tall, skinny, with red hair. Looks like a scarecrow put him together."

Realizing Croydon was following the same group he was, Grant-Merchant stopped himself from correcting his old friend. Croydon was a good chap but he was impossible when it came to differentiating between Japanese and Chinese. Telling him about Miss Fukushima, however, would reveal Grant-Merchant's purpose.

By the time Grant-Merchant had made that decision, Croydon had run off, leaving the Major to consider the possibilities of just slipping through the door into the theater when no one was looking. Only the big, heavy-set, slightly stupid looking doorman made him stay where he was. Besides Croydon would be back soon with reinforcements. It was a more direct solution than he'd originally planned but it should still end with Miss Fukushima once more in military custody. And this time, Grant-Merchant promised himself, he'd find out just what that sneaky wench was up to.

Chapter Fifteen
Refreshments are Supplied Together with Hot Towels

Bai She finished his song and allowed himself to be forced off stage by the actor playing the monk. His mother wouldn't have found his present occupation as humorous as he did, but her tale had been told in very many places and for a very long time. Here in China it had taken a different form entirely from the one he'd been born to.

His mother would probably object more to his performing at all, but there wasn't much choice. He needed time to recover his strength from that damned centipede poison. The rapt attention of an audience wasn't exactly the faith his kind needed most, but it was an acceptable substitute. In some ways it was also hilarious.

Another source of amusement were all the interesting things his shadows were showing him. Sentient beings in their own right, they had a mischievous streak. Learned, no doubt, from his own. Of the eight, one was back in Khaitan keeping a shadowy eye on his lands and his current priestess. The rest remained nearby, wandering around poking curious 'noses' into places Bai She couldn't go. Or shouldn't, he reminded the one before it could do what it was considering. The actress playing Green Snake was a nice, polite, young lady and there was no excuse for visiting her dressing room uninvited. The last time had gotten Bai She slapped and deservedly so.

The others were wandering the audience, listening to conversations, poking critics and generally being small nuisances. Fortunately, with all those people and all the lights from the stage, no one noticed that some of the shadows around them had minds and wills of their own. Not to mention an odd resemblance to Bai She himself.

Two of his shadows were doing more serious work, attending to secrets their possessors would never share with Bai She. Both the Japanese soldiers and the Warlord of *Chinglung* Mountain were part of this whole convoluted mess surrounding the living metal and he needed to know everything he could, even if he was still too weak to do much about it himself.

Zhao having the metal wasn't good news. That he was apparently negotiating for its sale was slightly better, as it meant the warlord had no idea how priceless the stuff really was. Not that most of those trying to capture it knew either. As near as Bai She could tell, the only one with the remotest comprehension of its nature and its full power was Mudan and that only because it'd revealed itself to her. At least that meant she was treating it well. Like its creator, living metal was temperamental stuff.

As if thinking about Mudan was enough to summon the girl, Bai She noticed her sitting at the front of the theater with her companions. The show was almost over; leaving him to wonder what had brought them there. Whatever the reason, it was a convenient chance. He sent one of his shadows to tell Shen what he'd learned and what must be done.

Having no more part to play on stage, the rest being focused on the scholar and the monk, Bai She went back to the dressing room to clean off his face paint. To his surprise, he found most of the theater's company, those not involved in the current scene, standing at attention before a newcomer. Bai She hadn't met the man before, but there was something faintly familiar about him, even so.

"Ah," the stranger said. "You are our new actor."

"I am, although I'm afraid I cannot remain with the troupe," Bai She answered, inclining his head in a way that caused one or two of his fellow actors to murmur agitatedly. They expected more manners from someone in his position to this man. "You would be?"

"That's Master Dragon, Bai She! You can't talk to him like that."

Before Bai She could retort that he talked to everyone like that, the man called Dragon laughed softly. "Come. Let us speak privately."

They went aside and now Bai She was sure he ought to know the man, or why he was familiar. "Well?" he asked quietly.

"It must rankle, Lord of the Hidden River, to play your mother's role in a story that shamed and imprisoned her. It must rankle even more to be treated as a mere player in my theater, when you are a God in your own land."

Acknowledging the recognition, Bai She shrugged off the implicit apology. "I am no God, even in Khaitan. This body is too solid and real for that. As for the story? All things change, stories most of all. Madam White Snake's plight in China is not the same as my mother's. What is true here is not true there."

"I see." Thoughtfully, Master Dragon examined a stage prop sword, swinging it around himself carefully to test its weight. "What do you think of the story? What should the monk have done, faced with his student's defiance and a devil's desire for love?"

Bai She sighed, uncertain why he was being asked such a question. "I am my mother's son and born of that love," he pointed out. "Nor am I your God to be telling you the path that you must take. It does not work that way."

The man watched him patiently for a real answer and Bai She relented. "It depends on what the monk loved more, the rules or the student who trusted him, obeyed him and yearned for his happiness only slightly less than he yearned for my mother's. In Khaitan, the monk's refusal to accept his student's desire wreaked havoc across my mother's lands. Here in China, the White Snake and the scholar broke long established rules of order. Who knows what that would have done, if they'd been allowed to persist?"

For a long moment Master Dragon was quiet. Then, "Lord of the Hidden River, I thank you. I know what I must do, now."

As the man left him, Bai She wondered if he'd said the right thing or caused more trouble for someone, somewhere. Or perhaps both?

〈〈〈

Ordinarily, Fukushima enjoyed Chinese theater but her worry over their situation made it difficult to appreciate the fine singing, dancing and acrobatics being displayed on stage. Under other circumstances she thought she'd be among those in the audience throwing white flowers at the feet of the man playing Madam White Snake. He'd brought an edge to the role she'd never seen before, as if he knew and understood the character almost as well as he understood himself.

All that must take a back seat to the fact that she was in a great deal more trouble than she'd intended. Her commander wouldn't blame her for failing under the circumstances, but she wished she'd been more adroit about getting McLeod alone. Not to mention her failure to realize that she wasn't the only one who wanted him. She ought to have expected Wugong.

Then there was the fact that she was now in the company of a man who could blow her cover entirely. He was one of the few outsiders who knew she was a double-agent, thanks to his impetuous decision to go after *Tōgō* Unit all those months back. She ought to have arrested him instead of helping him steal the map that showed him where to fly. She most certainly should not have joined him on the mission, acting both as his co-pilot in that freezing little deathtrap he'd stolen and as his bombardier when they reached the camp.

Zhanchi was a brilliant pilot, a brave man and the most honest person Fukushima had ever come across; and that last made him dangerous. Honest people, especially young gallants like Zhanchi, were terrible at keeping secrets. All she could do, however, was smile, watch the play and hope he held his tongue.

The show was almost over when Fukushima noticed movement towards the very back of the theater. With a sinking feeling she recognized Major Grant-Merchant, accompanied by a dozen burly policemen. All were scanning the crowd and she was certain they were looking for her and possibly the others.

Having been given seats very nearly to the front of the house, thanks to Mudan's connections, it would take a few minutes for their pursuit to find them. The question was, how to get past without being noticed? "Mudan? I think we need another exit."

Mudan looked back briefly and with a gesture to one of the vendors, bought a bag of salted plums. At the same time she spoke softly in Cantonese. The girl took her money and bowed slightly before going behind a curtain.

Meanwhile the play was just coming to an end. The scholar shaved his head to become a proper monk, blessed by his master, and the Green Snake curled up in mourning around the White Snake's prison while, from within, the White Snake sang a song praising Buddha and promising to wait for her freedom. As the actors bowed, a small troupe of youngsters all dressed up in miniature versions of the monkey king's costume and leaping about wildly, ran into the audience.

This was not the way Chinese theater usually worked, but the Fragrant Stone Players liked to break convention as often as possible. They were among the first to have female actors and among the first to perform plays outside the traditional works. The show was supposed to continue on to another play, "The Ruse of the Empty City", but instead it appeared the younger members of the troupe had rebelled and taken over the stage and the audience.

Food was thrown, hot towels passed overhead and a grand free-for-all ensued, to the great amusement of the audience, who expected such nonsense. That the youngsters' behavior also inconvenienced the police was, Fukushima guessed, not at all a coincidence.

"Come." The girl who'd sold Mudan the plums was suddenly there again and Mudan rose, drawing McLeod after her. She didn't bother to make sure the rest of them followed, but Fukushima didn't hesitate. Shen and Zhanchi were already on their feet, following behind as they evaded the children.

Within moments they were at a door hidden behind the same curtain the vendor had used earlier. It opened and they entered, walking backstage amid men and women busily preparing for the next show. A man's voice called out from the stage, "That is quite enough. I, the Golden Dragon of Fragrant Stone Mountain, command your obedience!"

Young voices taunted, chimes rang, and Fukushima saw a man dressed in Imperial finery, wearing dragon mask face paint, fighting in a desperate mock battle with the children. One by one he picked them up and tossed them backstage, until the last came running at him to crawl straight up his back. The two spun off the stage to the crash of cymbals and drums and the audience screamed their approval.

Mudan called Fukushima's name. "We do not have time to gawk," she said grimly. "Come." She walked further back behind the scenes, something about her posture saying that there were dozens, perhaps hundreds, of places she would rather be. Fukushima followed, wondering why Mudan seemed so afraid to face her own family.

《《《

Ordinarily, being backstage of a Chinese theater would have been exciting and distracting in ways Conall dearly enjoyed. It was the carnival atmosphere; the smell of face-paint, sweat and food, the sound of instruments banging away noisily, the sight of dozens of people running to and fro, half dressed in strange costumes, borrowing and stealing make-up and arguing over who should get the last orange in the basket. It was the smells, the colors, the lights, the sounds, all combining in a kaleidoscope of impressions.

Most importantly, it was a whole crowd of people, all focused on their own business and ignoring the gawky Westerner meandering through. All of which meant that he could stare around, listen to the sounds and not be expected to know what to say because everyone was too busy to ask him anything. It let him listen and learn without ever having to explain what he was thinking or how he felt.

Right at this moment, however, Conall was as focused as he'd ever been. He knew Mudan's moods. Knew her sharp temper, combined with a sense of humor she had to fight to keep anyone from noticing. Knew how carefully she cultivated her distant and superior air of knowing far more than she ever said. Right now she was scared, and Conall understood why. The man on stage might hide behind a mask but he was obviously Cheh Chang, Mudan's father.

Knowing Mr. Chang was surely furious at his daughter for defying him, and none too happy with Conall for being the reason for that defiance, Conall wondered how to get Mudan out of this mess. It was, after all, partly his responsibility. Somehow, he didn't think it coincidental that the play the Fragrant Stone Theater had put on was that particular one. Was the only answer to allow himself to be locked away from her, so she could properly obey her father like a good daughter should?

Conall's thoughts were interrupted by a familiar voice cursing. Looking up, he smiled, genuinely pleased. "Tan? I thought that was you back at the nightclub." Tan was one of Chang's best men back home. He was also a friend, thanks to the times they'd worked together on some of Chinatown's various engineering projects. No doubt Chang had brought him along when he'd come after his wayward daughter. "What's wrong?"

"McLeod. I'd say it's good to see you, but I'd get in trouble for it." Tan grinned. "Also, I can't get this damned trap door to work."

Realizing they were near the back of the theater, standing in a large storage room, Conall saw Tan was trying to turn a hook on one of the support columns. Another of Chang's Lieutenants—Fu—was stamping on a section of floor while his partner, Chi, looked on disapprovingly. "Let me look," Conall offered.

"I was hoping you'd say that."

"Better hurry," Fu suggested. "Those police will be back stage soon and you're the ones they're looking for."

At a guess, that meant this was intended to be their escape route. Conall went to the support column and examined the hook, then—borrowing a knife from Chi—levered off the panel that hid the workings beneath. As he'd thought, "A gear's slipped." He fiddled with it, aware that he was garnering an audience. "Mudan, do you have a hair pin?"

She handed him one silently, removing the white peony she'd worn to match her evening dress. As he took it, working the metal between the gears to get the twisted one back in place, he asked, "Did I remember to tell you how lovely you look?" He wasn't sure. The last few hours had been so chaotic and there'd been so many distractions.

"Several times, Conall."

"Good. Because you do. Look lovely, that is."

She looked at him with that expression that mixed a desire to smack him with a yearning to giggle and he hoped he'd made her feel better about the situation. There wasn't much to be done about her father and there was no point in borrowing trouble when they already had enough. "Thank you, Conall," was all she said.

The gear slipped back into place and Conall tried twisting the hook. This time the flooring of the elevator shifted an inch before coming to a complete halt again. Conall eyed the angled surface thoughtfully; guessing all Fu's pounding had skewed it. He could hear the gears trying to turn and knew he'd better fix it quickly.

"Sometimes you need finesse and sometimes," he slammed his foot down on the higher end of the board, "you need to give a troublesome machine an attitude adjustment."

The floor shifted flat and slid down into the darkness, revealing a ladder. Conall was about to climb down when a voice spoke from the other side of the room. "Wait. There are things that I must say."

Conall looked up and realized Cheh Chang had entered. He'd doffed the mask and taken off the yellow robe he'd been wearing, revealing a ratty-looking business suit beneath. As always, his expression revealed nothing as he approached them. Mudan, on the other hand, was nearly white as a sheet.

Without hesitation, Conall stepped forward, "Sir, I know it's the last thing you want to hear, and something you may never agree to, but I love your daughter and I know she loves me. Please, despite law and custom, I once again beg you for her hand in marriage."

Chang looked dourly at Conall and said warningly, "California law…."

"Can go hang. I want to be with her and whatever you ask of me, if it is in my ability, I will give."

Without bothering to answer, Chang went to Mudan and looked directly into her eyes. To her credit, despite her state of mind, despite knowing she'd disobeyed him in spirit, despite knowing how angry he had to be, she faced him, her chin held high with that expression that said she regretted nothing. "Father."

"Daughter."

"I love you. I will always respect you. But this is a thing that matters to me." She reached out and automatically, Conall took her hand, though he had to move several steps to reach her. "I love him."

Slowly, Chang said, "I do not approve. I am not pleased." The same things he'd said before, the last time Conall had asked to marry Mudan. Then, in a gentle tone, he continued, "Whatever you choose, I accept. You are my daughter and what I desire most, in all the world, is your happiness."

Mudan stared at him and Conall felt her icy cold fingers tremble in his. Then she flung her arms around Chang and hugged him so tightly he squeaked. Only when she released him did he restore his dignity. "Now, go. You have much to do and little time in which to do it."

Chapter Sixteen
There is no Compulsory Registration of Deaths In Shanghai

It was past midnight when Soong got word that Zhao planned on selling the device he'd stolen to the highest bidder. By this time Soong was already furious: with Wugong, with his men and with the Eastern

" CONALL LOOKED UP
AND REALIZED
CHEH CHANG HAD ENTERED. "

Star's manager for allowing those nuisances from the Fragrant Stone Theater to wreak havoc on his dance floor.

Admittedly, all the guests had raved over the show, but Soong had had to grit his teeth throughout the whole thing. Wugong, the only person willing to listen to Soong gnaw fruitlessly on his anger, couldn't blame him at all. "I admit," he said when Soong stopped raging long enough to breathe, "I should have brought more men to take McLeod. I knew Striker's mistress would interfere if she got the chance." He still didn't know where the Japanese girl came in. Her behavior had shifted from spoiled mistress to competent fighter so quickly that she had to be an agent. For whom, however, he wasn't sure.

Soong turned on him. "You should have killed her, and the other woman."

Wugong had been about to, but, "McLeod got in the way. Since we need him alive, I didn't dare fire." He didn't explain how he'd lost his gun. That damned bracelet had turned on him and the admission was shameful. He'd no idea how the American had persuaded it to cooperate. It never had for him and that made him furious. How dare the little traitor accept the commands of a Westerner?

Slowly, Soong was regaining his equilibrium. "Where did that boy say the meeting was being held?"

"Willow Pattern Tea House." It was a good choice of venue. Surrounded by water and protected by guard spells so ancient and so often repeated they'd taken on a life of their own, it was impossible for sorcerers to use their powers against each other there. As for magical beings? They tended to run into trouble if they tried to enter. He said as much, adding, "I doubt the device will be with Zhao. He may not know how to use it, but he surely realizes it's magic."

"That doesn't mean we should ignore this meeting," Soong said firmly. "I want to know what happens." A dour smile lit his face as he watched his men cleaning up the remains of the party. "In fact, this will be a splendid opportunity. We can find out who was willing to pay the most for the engine without having to involve ourselves in the negotiations."

That seemed an excellent idea to Wugong and he said as much. "We may even capture McLeod at last," he suggested. Even if it turned out they didn't need the man, Wugong didn't like being thwarted. As for that woman of Striker's—well she was dead as soon as an opportunity presented itself.

"See if you can find Zhi Lin. The silly wench's wandered off somewhere but if there's anyone who'd be useful for this job, it'd be her. Just tell her not to make any of her damned *tun* again. We need at least one or two buyers alive."

⟨⟨⟨

"I was getting a bit worried about you, Fukushima. You disappeared so completely last night. I was afraid I wouldn't see you again."

Fukushima bowed before sitting beside Lord William on the park bench and watching the early morning walkers go past. Sitting out in the open made it easy to tell if anyone was near enough to listen. They'd spent a great deal of time in this place in the past and Fukushima had come to like and respect the man. He wasn't her direct commander but he had, despite an apparent vague befuddlement and obsession with horses, a brilliant, observant and thoughtful mind.

"You weren't hurt, I hope? I saw those men draw their guns on you, before they were interrupted. And I'm almost sure I heard a shot."

"There was shooting, but no one was hurt. Soong's man, Feng Wugong, was also interested in McLeod." Ruefully, she added, "I underestimated Miss Chang's skills. I'm not sure which of us would win in a fight; it would depend on what we were fighting for. But I don't want to ever face her again as a threat to her fiancée."

That news startled Lord William but he set it aside as unimportant. "Were you able to talk to McLeod alone?"

"Not alone, no. But I think Mudan's connection with the Jeen Loon is purely familial. I took a risk and allowed her to be present while I spoke with him." Allowed was not accurate, but Fukushima didn't want to admit it. Now that Mudan's father had permitted Mudan and McLeod's marriage nothing would separate the two.

"What did he say? Did he understand what we want?"

"He told me that he hasn't been allowed to see the device and that as long as Mudan was safe, he had no reason to assist the Soong, or anyone, in any sort of scam. I believe him."

"About all we can ask for. Can't very well expect a civilian to steal the device." Lord William tossed some bread to a pair of wandering Mandarin ducks and continued, "I have news for you, too. Soong no longer has the thing."

Startled and dismayed, Fukushima asked, "The Japanese? The Chinese? Germans?"

"The Warlord of *Chinglung* Mountain, apparently."

Fukushima sat up straight and stared at Lord William. That was terrible news. Zhao Zhu had a small army, an impenetrable base and a deadly reputation. Before she could say a word, Lord William added, "He doesn't appear interested in keeping it. He's selling it to the highest bidder, on the presumption that those who were prepared to buy it from Soong will buy it from him instead. He's probably right."

It still wasn't good, but selling the device meant Zhao couldn't use himself. Whether that meant it was actually useless or that he didn't have the technological capabilities needed to deal with it was another question entirely. "How did you find out?"

"He sent a man to Sir Bruce. There's to be a meeting at the Willow Pattern Teahouse. Sir Bruce had quite the fit over it and refuses to attend, so I'll be going instead. I'd count it as a favor if you found a way to be there, too."

Given Zhao had probably asked everyone interested in the engine to be there and given their mutual distrust and—in some cases, outright hatred—there was nothing that would keep Fukushima away.

《《《

Zhi Lin examined her handiwork with pleasure. This was what she'd trained for, the careful presentation of a meal fit for an Emperor, combined with the skilled concealment of deadly traps that, if required, would end the life of their victim in seconds. The latter were only necessary if her master's guests were fool enough to use force to get what they desired.

Those guests weren't due until noon, but already the expected, but uninvited ones, had arrived. Her father had hired the teahouse and set his own men to man it for the duration of the meeting but now his servants weren't the only ones inside. Already ten members of Soong's gang had infiltrated the place and she expected there'd be more.

They were the ones her traps were prepared for but, cat-like, she chose to wait until all her prey was within range. Darts would fly, poison filled candles would scent the air, and blood, she promised herself, would spill. The abuse and shame she'd experienced over the last few days would be wiped away.

Noticing a stranger approaching the teahouse, Zhi Lin fought back irritation and stood in the door, blocking his path. He was a tall, older, Chinese man dressed in a ratty old suit, his bare feet stuck in sandals and his grey hair thick and messy. Even if the place hadn't been closed for a private party he hardly looked the sort to be welcomed. The only thing about him that suggested he was more than he appeared was his ebony cane with a gold dragon head. As he came a bit closer, she realized his suit, while old and tattered, concealed a fine silk shirt. A gem worth more than a pound of opium glittered in his tiepin.

Before Zhi Lin could open her mouth to stop the man, he snapped, "Don't get in my way, missy. I'm here for a meeting."

"I greatly doubt that you were invited to any such thing. My master has hired the teahouse and I know everyone who has been invited."

"I suggest you examine your list more carefully, Miss Zhao. I am Chang Cheh, the owner of Jeen Loon Enterprises."

Zhi Lin opened her mouth, then closed it and opened it again. "You are Chang Cheh?" His name was, indeed, on the list of invitees, her father having learned of the man's presence in Shanghai earlier that morning. Slowly she decided to accept the claim, if only for sake of the silk shirt and the ebony cane. And the imperial jade studded tiepin, she realized, looking closer. "Mr. Chang, I apologize, but the meeting is not until after noon. I cannot invite you in to negotiate ahead of the others. That would not be fair."

"Then I shall sit downstairs and enjoy the famed view and air of the Willow Pattern Teahouse. If you are not too busy to sit with me, I shall even enjoy your company."

She might have argued, but a glance down the street gave her a sharp twinge of worry. She'd planned for trouble from all sorts of directions but not this one. Why, she wondered, were the Shanghai Police wandering the Old City and why did it appear they were headed straight for the teahouse?

"Mr. Chang, I hardly have any time to sit and chat, with so much still to do. But if you wish to rest on the patio, I will bring you tea and let you enjoy the atmosphere." She took Mr. Chang's arm and led him inside, closing and locking the door behind her. As long as she was careful about it, she should be able to keep the old fool from noticing her murdering Soong's men. Disposing of the bodies would be more difficult with the police keeping watch, but that was what trapdoors over deep ponds were for; getting rid of the refuse.

ᕦᕦᕦ

"Damn it! That woman saw us and just closed right up!"

Major Grant-Merchant looked at his friend Croydon and tried not to show his annoyance. "I did say it'd be better to send your men in undercover."

"I can't. I got word this morning that some fellow named Zhao hired the place. They're not letting anyone inside without an invitation. Bloody suspicious, I call it!"

Grant-Merchant wondered if his friend was using his head at all. "If that's the case, marching on the place without a warrant just makes us all look like bloody fools. It was a silly idea, that's what it was." Now he regretted involving himself with an enterprise that probably had nothing to do with that Fukushima girl. It was only because he shared Croydon's annoyance over her escape that he'd joined the venture.

Croydon snorted. "That Chang fellow doesn't have a place to go. The teahouse being in the middle of a pond like that makes sure no one can just slip out a window. I'll put half my men on front and go to the back. There's a servant's entrance we can use. No harm in looking around, you know."

Trailing along with Croydon, Grant-Merchant reflected that his friend's desire for a coup that would get him out of Shanghai was blinding him to sense. Granted, rumor had it that Cheh Chang was the leader of a criminal organization hidden behind his shipping company. Granted, Mudan Chang was neck deep in a questionable situation. Granted she and her companions had escaped Croydon's grasp and embarrassed him horribly by doing so. None of that made following the fellow into what was obviously a private meeting a good plan.

The Willow Pattern Teahouse was a big building with several smaller ones behind it. Built at the center of a deep pond, it was a favorite of both tourists and locals. The main building was two stories, surrounded by a patio, while the smaller buildings behind contained the kitchen and storage rooms. As they came around towards the back, Grant-Merchant saw Cheh Chang sitting outside, peacefully reading a newspaper and sipping at a cup of tea.

They went into the kitchen, where the smell of garlic and onion was nearly overpowering. Something was simmering on the stove and one of Croydon's men seemed unable to resist dipping a finger in and tasting it. "Damn, that's some good stuff," he said and was roundly scolded.

Finding no one there, they continued through to the main building. Oddly, no one was there to argue with them. The place appeared empty, except for the old man sitting outside. Croydon glared through the open doorway at Chang. "What is he up to?" he demanded. "This must be some scheme of his."

The old man answered in a cheerful tone, his English almost too perfect. "Oh, no. This is not my scheme at all. I am merely here as an interested observer. You are right to think there is trouble, however, and of a sort I do not believe you are prepared for. If you value your life and the lives of your men, you would do well to turn around and go home. This place is a trap meant for others, but it will eat you alive as well."

Even as he spoke, Croydon's man, the one who'd tasted the stuff in the kitchen, suddenly grabbed his throat and, after one choked cry, fell twitching to the floor.

Chapter Seventeen
Don't Worry, Your Guide Will Take You There Anyway

"I cannot enter with you," Shen warned as he brought his car to a halt near a set of large buildings that were, as Conall's guidebook had promised, built atop a set of columns at the center of a pond. "There are spells that interfere with mine and while I could bypass them, there'd be no point. I am not, after all, invited."

Conall gazed at the building curiously. Legend, again according to the guidebook, had it that the Willow Pattern Teahouse was the model for the art on the famed willow pattern china and it did bear a striking resemblance. When he said so, Mudan looked at him indulgently and said, "Yes, my dear."

Ignoring their by-play, Shen continued as if Conall hadn't spoken, "It would be just as well for Zhanchi to remain with me." He pointed at another car, parked a short distance away. Murtagh's vehicle, Conall realized.

"He won't be pleased to see me," Zhanchi agreed. "And we can't attend the meeting anyway." The last was a reminder to Shen that, despite everything that proved otherwise, he was still—officially—just a cab driver.

Shen inclined his head in silent agreement before getting out to assist Mudan from the car. Once Conall had joined her, he drove off around the corner behind the teahouse, no doubt to park where they wouldn't be seen.

Now they were there, Conall wondered if this was such a good idea after all. He worked for Striker and the only reason he'd be expected to look at that engine would be if the British-Oriental Consortium won their bid. Still, Striker had asked him to come for moral support and he'd agreed, even though he'd much rather be back at the Jeen Loon safe house with Mudan.

Automatically, he slid his hand around Mudan's, still giddy over the fact that the two of them had finally persuaded her father to let them marry. It wasn't going to be easy: society was against it from both sides of the tracks. It was, however, the thing he wanted most and all that kept him from shouting his happiness to the world was the fact that Mudan would probably find a way to quiet him. Wise woman that she was, it wouldn't be with a kiss, either.

They approached the teahouse together, Conall's eyes scanning everything with avid interest. Even distracted by his impending marriage and everything else, he couldn't help observing his surroundings. The Old City was an attractive place, reminding him in many ways of the older part of Strikersport's Chinatown. Colorful tile, little statues and carvings, windows covered in rice paper; all delightfully different to his eyes. There was a wonderful smell in the air, a combination of garlic and onions, with a note of ginger and charbroiled meats. Soft chimes rang, jingling musically at every passing breeze. Well, almost musically. "They could retune that one," he couldn't help saying, pointing at the offending chime.

"That is another person's problem," Mudan answered as they went through the big red-lacquer doors. When he noticed Mr. Chang sitting idly by on the porch she whispered, "He will not interfere, but he told me this morning that he wishes to know Zhao's plans." She nodded to her father, who began folding his newspaper in preparation to join them.

A familiar woman came down the broad staircase towards the middle of the room. Dressed in a gown of dark blue velvet and fur, there was a decadence to her appearance that belied her occupation only two nights earlier. It was a good thing that Sir Bruce wasn't joining them. If he was already furious over the theft of the device he would be even angrier to realize their hostess was the same cook whose *tun* fish had nearly killed him.

Zhi Lin bowed, although the look in her eyes when she saw Mudan was filled with hate. "Greetings. You are the last to arrive. Will you follow me? General Zhao cannot, alas, join us, but he has commanded a banquet in honor of his guests."

"With less opium and *tun*, I trust," Mudan said coolly. "Or any other of what I am certain is a diverse arsenal?"

"It would be the grossest of insults to provide our invited guests so much as a taste of such things, Miss Chang."

Conall noticed the slight emphasis on invited and couldn't help asking, "And where do Mudan and I stand in that category?"

"You are both members of Mr. Striker's party, Mr. McLeod. You need have no fear on that count." Zhi Lin answered.

"And on that note," Mr. Chang said as he joined them on the stairs, "I suggest we waste no more time in pleasantries. There is food to be had and I, for one, have spent a hungry hour enjoying the aroma of cooking almost as good as yours, daughter."

While Mr. Chang was likely right, Conall had a feeling his future father-in-law had not endeared himself to Zhi Lin by saying so.

《《《

Bai She hesitated a moment at the edge of the pond surrounding the Willow Pattern Teahouse. The place was protected by a powerful and ancient spell that made the use of hostile magic difficult. It was also designed to prevent those for whom magic was part of their being from entering under any form but their natural one. All because the owner of the house had lost his daughter to a fox spirit, centuries ago.

The spell had been reset daily for hundreds of years, until it was inextricably embedded in every solid surface surrounding the teahouse. The trouble with such spells, however, was that they tended to become so rigid that it was possible to slip past chinks in its design, if one was sufficiently supple or powerful enough. Luckily for Bai She, he was both.

Slithering around the pond in his serpent form, Bai She quickly became aware of the scent and taste of death in the water. Some came from cooking refuse, old bones rotting away in the very depths of the pond and mostly belonging to oxen, pigs or sheep. Disturbingly, the most recent bodies were human. His shadows couldn't join him in the darkness below the teahouse, but he didn't need them to. He could taste gunpowder, telling him these men had been armed. He also recognized poison, and when he slid along one corpse he felt a dart buried in its neck.

When one lived as long as Bai She, death became an old companion. Even so, it was one he didn't care for. He especially didn't like the cutting off of all too short lives too soon. Murder, and this was nothing else, was something he highly disapproved of. Even if, as he suspected, these victims had been gangsters and probably guilty of other killings in their time, he didn't like it at all.

Realizing he'd become distracted, Bai She circled round, searching for a way inside. The bodies were all gathered in one area, directly beneath one of the outbuildings. There had to be a trap door just above the water here. No way the murderer would just dump their victims in the pond from one of the walkways.

The trap door was closed and latched, but there was sufficient light inside the room above for Bai She's shadows. One or two alone couldn't have moved the latch, but all seven together could and did. Pushing the trap door open with his nose, Bai She slithered up into a storeroom that stank of opium. He shifted form and was about to head for the teahouse itself when a noise drew his attention.

"Now how did I miss your being here?" he asked, using his shadows' sight to examine the dozen or so policemen sprawled on the floor of the storeroom. The smell of opium was strongest near them and he realized they'd been drugged into unconsciousness. Only one moved, a middle-aged man who looked like a soldier. His eyes were on Bai She, wide and dimly terrified through his opium induced delirium. "And why didn't the murderer kill you, as well?"

The one man who might have been able to answer didn't, possibly because it was too much for him to manage after watching a giant white snake transform into a man. Worried the murderer would be back to finish the men off, Bai She sent one of his shadows out to find Shen. His partner wasn't strong enough to pass the spell protecting the teahouse but his acolyte was entirely human. The lad could put that strong back to use to help get these poor fools out of danger.

It wasn't long before Zhanchi appeared in the doorway. Everything about him, from posture to scent, spoke of apprehension. "Shen said you wanted help?"

"I do," Bai She agreed, indicating the men around him. "I don't have time to waste, but we can't leave these people here. Assist me in getting them out."

Zhanchi obeyed without argument, pleasing Bai She. The boy might demand answers later, but right now he obviously knew not to pester someone with questions when there was work to do. He couldn't speak for Shen, of course, but the ability to put off curiosity until it was more convenient was a trait Bai She valued.

It took several trips. Bai She was still weak and could only manage one man at a time. Zhanchi could have carried two at once, but the bridge was too narrow for him to do so safely. Still, within a short while they'd gotten everyone moved to Shen's car, Bai She handing his off to Zhanchi at the edge of the spell surrounding the teahouse.

Once they were done, Bai She paused to count heads. With a sinking feeling he realized one was missing; the soldier, the only one who'd been awake enough to open his eyes. He must have managed to escape, either out of fear of Bai She or determination to complete his mission.

"Well," Bai She grumbled to himself, heading back inside, "I suppose I'll have to rescue him, too."

《《《

"I am surprised, deeply surprised, to learn you are allowing your daughter to marry that foreign devil."

"It was, I felt, for the best."

"Didn't you mean her to marry that boy Tan? The one you've been raising as your lieutenant?"

"I hoped they would marry. I did not set my heart on it. Perhaps if they were closer in age they would have become closer in other ways."

"Even so… a *gweilo*…."

"A most clever and capable *gweilo*. I have every reason to believe they will prosper."

Mudan kept her face still as Mr. Tsao and her father discussed her future. They were speaking in Chinese and the other guests, with the possible exception of Lieutenant Kurumata, didn't understand. Just as well, too, she reflected. The American representative, Mr. Church, surely knew such marriages were forbidden under California law.

Fortunately, the other guests were ignoring the Chinese guests and pretending to be friendly over the huge and delicious banquet Zhi Lin had provided. Fish, pork, chicken, great tureens of soup, great platters of noodles and vegetables and, to top the whole thing off, a melon filled to the brim with a soup made from the very best the sea had to offer. The smell alone was incredible and enough to make anyone forget their manners. Mudan was just glad Zhi Lin had been truthful about there being nothing harmful in the food.

Instead of listening to the discussions around her, Mudan paid close attention to the way her father's fingers twitched. Every movement had meaning and he was telling her what he'd seen since his arrival earlier that morning. Policemen being knocked unconscious, one possibly killed. Men from the Soong gang, disguised as waiters, cut down as silently and unobtrusively as could be. He'd pretended to be oblivious, but as far as he could tell, the entire building was under Zhao's control. Most importantly, although Zhao had claimed he wouldn't be at the meeting, he was the man calling himself Tsao.

Tsao had been introduced as a representative of Chiang Kai-Shek. If he was really Zhao he'd either taken the real Tsao's place without anyone noticing, or had always been Tsao. He was apparently confident that Mudan's father wouldn't dare betray the truth, lest Zhao reveal too much about Jeen Loon's activities.

'It isn't so much not daring as being too curious,' Mudan's father's fingers told her, 'He's playing a bit too close to my territory and I would know what he plans.'

It was Mudan's father's usual way; allow the enemy to overreach themselves, then, when they thought they'd grasped the prize, pull it and the rug out from under them. Mudan made a gesture of understanding and watched the latest platter be carried in. Several huge ducks, roasted to obvious perfection, sat atop a mound of dark brown sauce that had a strange, spicy, sweet, scent to it. Cloves, cinnamon, cardamom, turmeric and far more nutmeg than Mudan had ever dared use. So much, in fact, that she wondered if it were healthy. What was it her mother had told her about the stuff? She wished she could remember.

Zhi Lin smiled at her. "There is no need to worry," she said in Chinese. "There is nothing in this food that you would not use yourself."

"Perhaps, but in far lesser quantities," Mudan began, watching the servants bring clean plates to Zhi Lin so she could serve the duck. Something felt wrong but she simply didn't know what. Perhaps it was Zhi Lin's expression that made her uncertain? And was that because Zhi Lin had done something to the food or because she wanted Mudan to think she had?

Without reason to stop the others from eating, Mudan would have simply claimed to be too full to accept more than the smallest portion. Her intention became a moot point when a strange man came stumbling into the room. He was a Westerner, sandy-haired and mustached. He was also vaguely familiar and after a moment Mudan remembered that he was the man with Officer Croydon the night before.

From the looks of him, he'd been knocked out and dragged around. His tie was twisted around his neck, his shirt was pulled half out of his trousers and his hair was standing on end even more than Conall's sometimes did. He grasped the door, staring wildly at the dinner guests. Then he rushed at the platter in front of Zhi Lin and knocked it to the floor. "Don't… don't eat…," he gasped. "It's poison!"

Chapter Eighteen
The Chief Attraction at Lunghua is the Pagoda

Zhanchi caught up with Bai She as he reached the first step leading to the upper level of the teahouse. He was just in time to hear the sound of something crashing above them and someone yelling something about poison. Bai She muttered, "Well, that's torn it," and raced up the steps, his braids jangling around him and his shadows leaping and diving in imitation of the wild dance of the monkey children from the night before.

They reached the large dining room where the meeting was being held just as several of the waiters caught hold of the man Bai She had been following. Before anyone could speak, Bai She said, "I cannot apologize enough for this rude interruption. Allow me and my companion, please, to take this poor madman away so he might disturb you no more."

Zhanchi, taking Bai She's hint, quickly went to the Westerner's side and held him up gently. "He's eaten something that disagreed with him," he told the group, aware of Murtagh's indignant expression and doing his best to ignore it. Before the Englishman could protest a group of men Zhanchi recognized from the night before burst into the room.

"What?" Zhi Lin said, sounding utterly disgusted. "Didn't I get all of you pests?"

"You murderess! I saw you kill those men!" the Englishman shouted wildly.

Zhanchi's brother grinned at Zhi Lin, waving his fan in a casual sort of way. "You didn't think I'd be that obvious, did you? Those were just underlings. I figured you'd have the place trapped." He didn't see the expression of cold dislike Bai She turned on him, or he would have been a great deal less confident.

"Killer! She's a killer!"

Lord William rose to his feet, glaring at Zhanchi. "I demand an explanation. Who are you and what are you doing with Major Grant-Merchant?"

"At the moment," Mr. Chang said, smiling in a way that made his kinship to Mudan obvious, "I believe he is rescuing the poor man."

Zhanchi scanned the room, seeing mostly familiar faces. Mudan and Conall looking as if they'd like to leave. Mr. Chang and another Chinese businessman, this one older, balding, with broad features and a broken nose. An oddly familiar Japanese. Striker and another man who looked to be American by his clothes and attitude and another Englishman besides Murtagh. All of them, with the exception of Conall, Mudan and—probably—Mr. Chang, interested in gaining control of that engine of Soong's. And, of course, Wugong and Zhi Lin, along with men probably armed with everything they could manage to carry.

The Major stared wildly around the room, still trying to point out Zhi Lin's perfidy. Then his eyes fell on the man sitting beside Mr. Chang. "You! I know you! This is your work."

Lord William stared at his fellow Englishman. "Grant-Merchant, what the devil are you talking about? That's Mr. Tsao, a reputable teak dealer."

"Tsao?" the Major scoffed. "That may be the name he gave you, but I know who he is. China's crawling with his sort and he's the worst of them. That's General Zhao Zhu, the Warlord of *Chinglung* Mountain!"

The man smiled in a friendly sort of way as everyone stared at him. "Zhi Lin, daughter, is our exit prepared?"

"It is, sir."

Zhao, and it had to be he, rose to his feet and went to his daughter's side. "It seems negotiations are, for the moment, at a standstill. I would have preferred to complete them here and quickly, but it seems that is no longer possible."

Wugong raised his hand as if to fling his centipedes, then stopped with a frustrated growl. "I swear, I'll kill you."

"That will be difficult, Mr. Feng, for in one short moment I will no longer be here." The warlord looked over the group. "If anyone still desires the device I hold, come to *Chinglung* Mountain to tell me what you will give for the privilege. I suggest you be swift, however, because I may just decide to make use of it myself."

Before anyone could open their mouths to object, a swirl of deep blue-black smoke filled the room. When it was gone, so was Zhao and Zhi Lin.

⟨⟨⟨

Conall rose to his feet and quickly examined a spot on the wall near the door. The others were babbling angrily, Wugong shouting threats, Lord William and the others demanding answers. Only Murtagh sat quietly, fingers pinched on the bridge of his nose as if he had a headache.

At last, after a minute of searching, Conall found what he was looking for. Both Zhi Lin and her father had been standing together at the other end of the room. The servants, who had used the smoke to escape, were standing nearer to the exit and Conall had noticed one make the slightest of motions just before Zhao's escape.

"What is it, Conall?" Mudan asked, joining him.

"That wasn't magic."

Conall's statement caused everyone to stare at him, except Bai She, who simply smiled. Some, of course, were skeptical that he'd even suggest such a thing as magic existed. Those who knew it did were surprised he thought Zhao hadn't used it. Except, of course, for Bai She. Conall suspected he already knew.

Finding a spot among the carvings around the door frame, Conall pointed to the floor where Zhao and Zhi Lin had stood. "Watch." When he flipped the switch, the flooring dropped away, revealing a dark crawlspace beneath. "They've probably escaped by now. No way that doesn't lead to a quick exit."

Bai She agreed. "I considered stopping them, but they were cornered and the girl has far more poisons on her than I care to deal with." He went and took Major Grant-Merchant from Zhanchi, adding, "Someone should get the Major to the hospital. As I can't leave the city yet, I'm best for that job. I'd suggest you lot decide what you're going to do."

"And why should we listen to a theater actor with delusions of power?" Kurumata asked grimly.

"You don't have to," Bai She said and he smiled maliciously at the Japanese Lieutenant. "I have nothing to do with you and yours. Nor do I wish to." He turned his attention on his charge. "Now then, sir, I believe we'd best be going. You have a long recovery ahead of you."

" A SWIRL OF DEEP BLUE-BLACK
SMOKE FILLED THE ROOM. "

As Bai She left, Zhanchi started to follow. Before he got more than a few steps, however, Murtagh snapped, "Where do you think you're going?"

"What?"

"We're going to need a pilot." Zhanchi turned disbelieving eyes on Murtagh, whose expression showed nothing of what he was thinking. "Zhao has a private airfield at his castle. I'm sure he'll be taking a plane there as soon as he can. We can't beat him home, but we can at least follow. It takes hours to get there by land and I, for one, am tired of all this fiddling around."

From the look on Zhanchi's face, the last thing he'd expected had been Murtagh forgetting, or ignoring, the fact that Zhanchi had abandoned his employer the night before. "But…"

"We'll discuss how much I dock your pay for yesterday's little fiasco later." Murtagh eyed Zhanchi disapprovingly, adding, "I hired you to fly. So, fly. In fact, go to *Lunghua* airfield right now and get a plane ready. And make sure you choose one big enough for all of us. Well, most of us. I draw the line at any of that lot." He gestured with his thumb at Wugong's men. "They can find their own way there, and probably will."

Before Zhanchi could open his mouth to argue, Conall decided it was time to get him, and Mudan, out of there. He took her hand as he said, "We'll go with you. You might need help getting the plane ready."

)))

Rather than involve himself in foolish arguments, Kurumata followed the Chinese pilot outside, where he and his companions climbed into a too pretty limousine. They were aware of him, or the girl was, for she glanced through the rear window as they drove away. Knowing their destination, he went to his own car and trailed behind them. He didn't care about the others, but he refused to be left behind.

To Kurumata's surprise, the car drew to a halt before it reached the airfield, stopping outside the famed *Lunghua* pagoda. Puzzled, he watched the occupants exit the vehicle and head for the temple beside the tall structure.

"What are they up to?"

The question made Kurumata turn and look behind him. "You? Fukushima? What are you doing here?"

"The same as you, keeping an eye on that lot." She got out of the car and he was startled to realize she was dressed in a waiter's outfit. Had she been there through that admittedly delicious meal? He hadn't noticed her at all.

"Where are you going?"

"They know me and trust me. I can go find out what they're doing. You should...." She broke off as Kurumata got out of the car and joined her. "Stay here."

"I want to know what they're up to, too."

Following the others into the temple, Kurumata realized they, or at least the man Murtagh had called Zhanchi and the woman, Mudan Chang, were making offerings at each of the shrines inside. They lit joss stick after joss stick, ending their pilgrimage at a statue of a dragon twisting around amid the blossoms of a flowering plum tree. It was carved gold and lavender jade and even Kurumata had to admit it was one of the most beautiful things he'd ever seen.

By now he was close enough to hear what was being said. Zhanchi had bowed his head and was praying softly. "You guided my hands before, Flowering Dragon. I beg of you, guide them again. Guard my wings. Loft me high. Carry me far."

The incense he placed in the sand in front of the statue flared brilliantly and soft purple smoke rose around the statue. Kurumata almost, almost, had a moment of superstitious fear. But if there were Gods here, they were small, fragile things, too weak to protect even one young and foolish worshipper, much less an old, decrepit and decadent country.

A voice whispered in his thoughts, "Do not be so sure of that, child of the Rising Sun. I have not forgotten and I am not ready to forgive what you and yours have done." He stared around, trying to find the source of the voice, but there was no one except Fukushima near him and the voice had been quite male.

Zhanchi turned to look at his companions, his expression a little embarrassed. "Thank you for letting me stop here," he said. "I never fly without visiting."

"I've no objection," McLeod said quietly. "You take what help you can from whatever place you can get it."

The limousine's driver inclined his head. "It's always wise to recognize your patron," he added. "But now that the proprieties have been satisfied, I think we'd best be on our way. There isn't much time to waste. Isn't that right, Lieutenant Kurumata? Miss Fukushima?"

Kurumata was surprised at the arrogance in a mere driver but before he could argue, or take offense, Fukushima bowed. "I think you're right, Shen. Lieutenant? Shall we go?"

He was about to agree when something made him look more closely at Zhanchi. "I keep thinking I know you from somewhere."

"I work for CNAC," the young man said. "Perhaps you were aboard one of the few flights they've allowed me."

Kurumata shook his head. "No. That's not it."

"Think on it later," Fukushima told him. "We have to go."

They returned to their cars and once again headed towards the airfield, Kurumata still pondering Zhanchi's strange familiarity. At last, deciding he wasn't going to remember, he asked Fukushima, "Did you hear someone in there? A man, making some sort of threat?"

"If you heard someone threatening us, why didn't you say something?"

"That didn't answer my question."

She looked at him curiously. "I didn't hear anything. What did the voice say?"

"Something about not forgiving or forgetting."

Fukushima mused, "It may have been someone talking elsewhere. Or, more likely, your imagination."

She was probably right, Kurumata mused. That place had an atmosphere and, frankly, an unwelcoming one. He didn't believe in Gods or demons anyway. Likely he was upset over the whole business back at the teahouse. Between having to listen to condescending Englishmen treating him like a clever child whose efforts to claim the whole of the East were a charming peccadillo and needing to keep his temper throughout the ordeal, he was completely out of sorts.

But, he reminded himself, it would soon be over. He would gain control of the device the Warlord of *Chinglung* Mountain had stolen and with it, bring himself, his family and his country the honor and glory that was rightfully theirs. And then those British idiots who thought Japan a mere toy they could put away when they were done with it would pay.

⟨⟨⟨

Chapter Nineteen
The Average Chinese is a Peaceable Fellow

When their plane reached *Chinglung* Mountain, they were greeted by a sight that sent chills up Zhi Lin's spine and set her master snarling. "What the hell happened here?" he demanded.

For a moment Zhi Lin thought the Japanese had followed through on their threat to simply bomb the castle. There were scorch marks everywhere and shattered timbers where something had landed and landed hard. Then she recognized the damage for what it was. "Raud. It had to be him."

Zhao landed the plane on the small strip on the south side of the mountain. "The Black Dragon you told me of? How dare he?" As he climbed out and looked up the hill at his castle, perched at its very peak and still looking quite safe and solid, he added, "Obviously he failed. My men must have driven him off."

A score of Zhao's men came running down the steps from the castle and stood at attention. "Welcome home, sir!"

"I see things have been… interesting."

"Sir."

"We'll go inside and you can report. I have guests coming and I need everything ready before they get here."

As soon as they'd reached the castle, Zhao waved Zhi Lin off. "Go find something to do, girl. I doubt that lot will want another of your meals after today."

She bowed, though it grated on her. She was the oldest and most loyal of Zhao's children and she had put her entire life into obediently following his commands. Yet in the end, all she was a no-account girl-child sent off to play while the adults worked. Only when her special skills were needed, and the only thing that would do, was she allowed to take part in her father's business.

The castle was huge, a tangled maze of passages that could be turned into a death trap. Even the living quarters could be dangerous if one didn't know what to touch before entering. Only the children's quarters lacked the darts, nets, spears, sliding walls and poison gas that protected the rest of the castle. Even Zhao knew one couldn't expect children to keep their poky little fingers out of places they didn't belong. He claimed it was a lesson he'd learned the hard way and when Zhi Lin had been small, she'd believed him. Even now, she wasn't sure he'd been exaggerating.

The children of *Chinglung* Castle were, mostly, the sons and daughters of Zhao's soldiers. They were kept there for Zhao's safety, rather than their own. As long as the General had their children in his hands, hidden away at the center of a maze of deadly traps, his men would remain loyal to keep them safe. They were both carefully protected guests and hostages to their fathers' loyalty.

When Zhi Lin entered the communal play room, she came to a dead halt and stared at the man sitting at the center, juggling knives that glittered as they rose and fell, the children watching him play with rapt attention. "Oh, hello Miss Zhao. Long time no see." It was Chen Tang, grinning like the fool he was.

She glared at him for his arrogance. "What are you doing here? How did you get in?"

"Aunt Zhi Lin!" One of the girls, the one she'd been teaching to cook, came running to her. "Chen Tang saved the castle! He was great! We watched it through Third Wife's scry glass! He waited until the Black Dragon was almost on top of him and slung a bomb stone right in its mouth!"

When Zhi Lin looked at Chen sharply, he shrugged and grinned, putting his knives away one by one. "I like to keep my hand in with the sling-bow. It was the least I could do, seeing I came here for other reasons entirely."

"To rob us, you mean."

"Though honesty causes me great pain, I admit it."

"You will never get into my father's vault."

Chen tossed something to her. The beaded necklace her father had claimed from the last Emperor before he'd been banished to Manchuria. "You were saying?" He grinned, adding, "You might feed your centipedes and scorpions better. They're eating each other. As for the snakes, they don't like cold weather. They were asleep. The toads are a nice, traditional, touch, but hardly dangerous. Now the lizards? Well, komodo dragons are impressive, but like snakes, they slow down in cold weather. You might consider having your five venom hall heated. As for the rest of the traps? You don't get to be as old as I am without learning a few things...." He paused, looked thoughtful, and added, "And forgetting quite a few more. The poison gas was unexpected. Fortunately, I can hold my breath for a very long time."

Zhi Lin was torn between anger and an unusual feeling of amusement. "Why didn't you take what you came for?"

"I told Soong I'd see if I could get in. I didn't tell him I'd steal what he wanted for him. Besides, I was in Shanghai to keep an eye on an old friend's daughter. I only agreed to check out your father's vault because my friend showed up unexpectedly." Chen shrugged. "Besides, I wanted to see what the vault was like. Now that I have, I'll just head back and see if I'm still needed."

"Old friend's daughter?" Zhi Lin asked, and cursed herself for letting her curiosity overwhelm her sense.

"You met her the other night at Sir Bruce's. Her father was worried that she was getting herself in trouble with someone he didn't want her seeing and asked me to make sure she didn't do anything too foolish."

That answered Zhi Lin's question and she said grudgingly, "You mean Mudan Chang? You may as well stay here. She's likely to be headed this way with that fiancée of hers."

"Fiancée? Oho, the old bastard finally gave in. Well, it was inevitable, really." Chen settled back and began juggling fruit, to the great pleasure of the children. "If that's an invitation to stay for a while, I suppose I can be persuaded. Got anything to eat? No *tun*. It was delicious, the other night, but I really prefer something simpler. A nice chicken, maybe?"

"I'll see what I can do." It wasn't until Zhi Lin was halfway to the kitchen that she realized Chen had been at Sir Bruce's party. The question was which of the guests had he been?

⟨⟨⟨

Fukushima watched the rest of the plane's occupants make their way up the steps to *Chinglung* castle. They were guarded by dozens of General Zhao's men and stared around the pine covered hillside as if they were tourists gawking at a particularly interesting attraction. Not that she could blame them, because the castle was quite a sight. Its grey stone walls and towers surrounded the crest of the mountain. Beyond that, one could see the huge stone and wood towers of the castle itself.

Waiting until the others had headed up the steep and twisting path; Fukushima slipped out of the plane and disabled the guards with a chop to one neck and a kick to the other. Then she considered her next move. Reaching the castle from here would be easiest by the stairs but she didn't want to be seen. She was about to start for the trees when a light hand touched her shoulder. She came close to elbowing Shen in the face for startling her, but managed to control the reaction. "Don't do that."

"Don't try those trees," Shen said in return. "The General's traps extend all around the castle."

"Then what do you propose I... we... do?" Like her, Shen had to conceal himself aboard the plane. She hadn't worked out how the driver fit into all this, but guessed that he was either with the Communists or the Nationalists. More likely the latter; he had the air of one born to nobility and the Reds hated his sort.

Shen considered his answer and finally said, "You have seen the dragon and know him for what he is." It was a statement, not a question, so all Fukushima did was agree silently. "The idea of magic may be a thing you don't understand, but it, like dragons, exists. If you will trust me, I will conceal both of us beneath an illusion. Only McLeod will know we're there."

The existence of magic was something Fukushima preferred to ignore. It bothered her, the same way a beast that could not possibly fly, much less breathe fire, did. It was a cheat, a breaking of natural laws, and she would have liked to do without it entirely. She knew he was right though and bowed her head. "Then if you will trust me to work with you, despite my ancestry, I will trust you."

With an indulgent smile, Shen told her as he snapped his fingers, "You, my dear, are American and I trust you to protect your land's interests as I protect those of Khaitan." The snap was followed by a slight shifting of light and color and when Fukushima looked down she couldn't see her body at all. "Be careful. It can be disorienting, being invisible to oneself."

He wasn't wrong, Fukushima reflected as they made their way up the stairs a short distance behind the others. She'd have asked questions, tried to learn just what Shen meant by Khaitan, but the illusion covering them didn't hide their voices. Still, she tried to think if she'd ever heard that name before. There was a city in the Taklamakan desert called Khotan, but that could hardly be enough of a power to send an agent all the way to Shanghai.

The group ahead of them consisted, for the most part, of all the men who'd been at the meeting at the teahouse. Lord William, Church, Gerard were at the lead, Striker and Murtagh just a step or so after them, determinedly climbing the steep steps as if afraid to be left behind.

Kurumata looked like he wanted to run ahead just to be first. As for Wugong, he was moving carefully, watching every step as if expecting one of General Zhao's famed traps to be sprung any moment.

The only ones uninterested in the destination were Mr. Chang, McLeod and Mudan and that was because McLeod was busy sightseeing and Mudan was busy keeping him moving, to her father's great amusement. Fukushima wished Mudan the joy of that man. It seemed to her that he would be profoundly irritating to any sane woman. His distractibility, air of general confusion and tendency to look like a baby giraffe trying to walk certainly irritated Fukushima.

Then there was Zhanchi, who seemed mostly interested in not letting Kurumata get another good look at him. Not that she blamed him. The Lieutenant would be violently displeased if he realized Zhanchi was the one who'd helped bombed *Tōgō* Unit all those months before. To say nothing of what he would do if he found out Fukushima's part.

By the time they reached the top of the stairs it was nearly sunset and the sky over West Lake was an almost unbearably beautiful shade of tangerine, mixed with reds, purples, blues and gold. McLeod paused to stare at it with wide, fascinated eyes, slowing the party enough that Fukushima and Shen were able to catch up. Fukushima caught his eyes on her and realized he'd done so deliberately. Unable to speak, she nodded.

"Get moving," one of the guards snapped, pointing towards the great gates leading into the castle's main courtyard, a large square of pale stone, lit by dozens of flaring torches and decorated with columns and statues. "You're wasting time."

They all walked inside and the gates closed behind them with an echo that felt like doom.

《《《

Zhanchi wasn't sure what worried him most. The fact that Mudan and Conall were treating this whole business like a honeymoon, even though they'd yet to actually marry? The fact that, whether piloting or driving, all he seemed to be was a chauffer? The fact that he was in the company of a man who, should he recognize Zhanchi, would happily slit his throat? Or perhaps it was the fact that they were standing in the courtyard of a man known for his cruelty?

His only comfort was the faint scent of plum blossoms that still surrounded him. No one had commented on the odor, so perhaps it was in his mind alone, but it was a reassuring scent. It gave him the sense that there was at least one being who cared for his safety, both physical and emotional. Had he time, he'd think harder on the subject, try to work out who or what that being was and why it mattered, but right now all he could do was hope he didn't draw attention to himself.

The doors to the castle were opening, revealing several dozen more armed guards and the man they'd come to see. He was dressed in yellow robes of heavily embroidered brocade, covered with Imperial dragons and lined with silk and fur. The top of his head was bald, surrounded by a fluffy rim of graying hair. His face was fierce, lined and dour, and his smile put Zhanchi in mind of a tiger examining his prey. Yet again he wondered if the thing they'd come for was worth the bother. If Wugong had abandoned the quest for a bad deal he'd have been sure it wasn't.

"Welcome, my guests. I would offer you food, wine, women, but I think the time for those things is long past." The General spoke in English so everyone could understand him, his British accent near perfect.

"That," Lord William said grimly, "is so beyond true that I won't even bother to discuss it."

"Good. I hate wasting time." The General looked at the group with a satisfied smile and murmured something to one of his men, who saluted and marched back inside. "Now, before we discuss the matter that brings us here, I believe there's someone missing."

"Eh?" Lord William asked, sounding puzzled.

"Sir Bruce."

"He's sulking at home," Murtagh snapped. "Don't worry about him."

Zhao chuckled. "Actually, I'm rather afraid he isn't." The man who'd gone back inside returned with two other men, dragging a bedraggled and furious looking Sir Bruce between them. His clothing was tattered, his hair was unkempt and there were black marks all around his mouth. It looked to Zhanchi like he'd tried to smoke one of those trick cigars the movies were so fond of. He was tied up, his mouth gagged, and if he could have spoken he would have set everyone's ears burning with his fury.

"Sir Bruce was foolish enough to try and take advantage of another's attack on my castle. He ran afoul of my traps and my men captured him." The General smiled, "Don't worry. Whatever else happens, I'll release him into your hands. But, for now, I'll just hold him here. In case one of you is considering something foolish."

Lord William looked troubled but seeing the weapons held to Sir Bruce's neck, his only choice was to answer, "Very well. Then let us get to the point, General Zhao. You have a thing we all want and are prepared to sell it. We've come to bid. I think it's time you proved the thing even exists."

"Oh, it does. But it isn't the General's to sell."

The voice that spoke was not General Zhao's, and everyone turned to see a skinny young man in black sitting on the head of one of the stone lions guarding the steps to the castle. He was grinning dangerously as he bit into a large steamed bun. He chewed slowly, deliberately, and finally swallowed. With his free hand he raised a jar filled with some strange silvery substance. An object attached to its lid released small charges of electricity into the bottle that crackled brilliantly. "You see?"

Another voice said, "You bastard, Chen! You said you didn't steal it!" Zhanchi realized Zhi Lin was standing at the door, watching the proceedings angrily.

"I implied I didn't, Zhi Lin. Besides, I'm a thief and a scoundrel. Lying is part of the job description." The man, Chen, waved off the accusation with an amused expression. "Good *cha siu bao* by the way."

"I should have poisoned it."

"Satisfaction would have brought me back," he retorted.

"You little bastard! What are you playing at?" "How dare you rob my treasury!?" That was both Wugong and Zhao. They glanced at each other angrily, and Zhao gestured at his men to grab Chen.

That proved far more difficult than expected. Chen was fast, agile and able to leap far higher and further than any one of the men chasing him. Jar tucked under one arm, he bounded from one end of the torch lit courtyard to another, finally landing atop a tall column no one else could climb. "I wouldn't play too rough," he pointed out, holding the jar out over the pavement below. "Wouldn't want me to drop this. You never know what might happen. It's been jostled quite a lot lately and I don't think it's in a very good mood."

It was Lord William who demanded, "What the devil do you mean, not in a very good mood?"

Chen's teeth flashed in a brilliant smile. "Lord William, you and your companions have been lied to. The engine Soong offered to sell you depends entirely on the contents of this jar." He raised a hand to keep anyone from interrupting. "Now, before everyone loses their mind, let me explain something. This is living metal, created by a mad God and imbued with a power beyond anything human science can understand—yet. It can't be reproduced in mass quantities, it quite literally has a mind of its own and it chooses its master. You have to earn its trust and I don't think there's more than one or two of you here who could do that."

Something drew Zhanchi's attention to Sir Bruce. He was twisting forward, shuddering as if he were in a fit. Somehow he tore the gag from his mouth and began screaming in a roar that seemed strangely familiar, "That's mine! Return it to me!" Wings burst from his back and his body suddenly transformed entirely to that of a huge and furious black dragon. With a single bite, he took off General Zhao's head. Then he let loose with a stream of flame aimed straight for Chen.

Without missing a beat, Chen leaped and twisted out of the flame's way, barely evading the dragon's attacks. At the same time Sir Bruce ripped his captors apart and leapt for the middle of the courtyard. "I will have what I desire. This land is mine to do with as I wish!"

Once again the dragon roared and everyone ran for cover, Zhanchi included. Then Sir Bruce reached out and snagged hold of Wugong. Zhanchi didn't hesitate. He didn't love his brother but Wugong was family and that mattered. He raced towards the dragon, not at all sure what he was going to do. Except burn, he realized as the dragon's mouth filled with flames.

Before the flames reached him, a tall figure blocked their path. Shen, appearing out of nowhere to protect him as he was trying to protect his brother. The fire surrounded Shen momentarily, charring him. As he crumpled to the ground Chen moved, drawing the dragon's attention by throwing a dagger straight for his eye. It missed, but made him the target again.

Horrified, Zhanchi leapt forward to Shen's side. "No," he said. "No. You promised me I'd fly. You can't be hurt. You have to keep your promise!" He didn't know why it mattered so much to him. Shen was just another man, a powerful sorcerer, but as mortal and frail as any other.

Then Shen's eyes opened from behind the dark charred surface of his skin and he smiled. "Yes," he said firmly. "I promised. And I keep my promises."

Slowly a wind swirled around Shen, smelling of plum blossoms and electricity. It gathered him up, a deep purple mist that rose high into the air. Someone was singing, crying out in a voice that thundered through the sky and drew clouds out of nothingness into a storm that flickered with lightning.

"Raud! Black Dragon of Sunderland! Invader! Thief! Murderer! Too long have you squatted in this land like a festering sore! Leave these mortals be! They are not your opponent! I AM!" The shout broke the air like a thunderclap as the Flowering Dragon, Shen transformed to his true shape at last, leapt on Raud and sank his jaws into the Black Dragon's shoulder.

Chapter Twenty
Private Flying is not Allowed

Mudan wasn't surprised when Shen changed. She hadn't been certain he was one of the many Immortal beings who haunted her ancestral lands but she'd suspected it. The two dragons rolled round the courtyard and she felt Conall drag her to the side. "We have to get out of here."

He was right, but the gate was closed and the guards were too stunned to do anything. Their master was dead and they'd no idea what to do. Nonsensically, and because she couldn't quite help it, she said, "See. Chinese dragons breathe lightning."

"They do," Conall agreed and she felt her father catch hold of her other arm to pull her to her feet. "It's quite impressive. No wings, either. How do they fly?"

"This is not the time," Mudan's father said. "You! Open the gate." His order, the only voice of authority, had the desired effect. Zhao's men reacted automatically, grabbing hold of the chains and pulling them. "Everyone! Get to the plane. You, girl, get your people to safety!"

Zhi Lin broke out of her terrified trance and, after a broken look at her father's corpse, nodded sharply. "Inside!" she shouted to her guards. "Those two are too much for you!"

Chen tossed the bottle he'd been holding to Mudan. "Take care of it," he shouted. "Chang, I'll help Zhi Lin if the dragon comes after her."

As Mudan wrapped her arms around the glass, Wugong appeared in front of her, rage filling his eyes. "*Gweilo!* Return that to me!" he shouted.

Tossing the jar to her father, Mudan caught hold of Wugong's outstretched wrist and twisted. As she torqued his arm forward, forcing him down, she brought her knee up into his chin. He struggled to break free of her grip and she glared into his eyes. "I am the insignificant and worthless daughter of the Golden Dragon. Not a white woman in disguise. Remember that the next time we meet, Feng Wugong." With that, she flung herself sideways and upwards, 'walking' up his torso and spinning. As her legs locked round his neck, she twisted around, flinging him over her as she spun. He hit the ground hard and lay still.

"Not so insignificant, nor worthless, as all that, my daughter," her father said. "In all things but one, you are most filial and I am most proud." He handed the jar back to her and gestured toward the gate. "Now. Run!"

The others were already leaving, but Murtagh still stood staring at the dragons with a stunned expression. "All this time, Sir Bruce was a dragon? You think you know a man and…."

"Murtagh, this is hardly the time!" Lord William snapped, grabbing his fellow Englishman by the arm.

Now they were all running and stumbling down the steps, Mudan clutching the bottle close in her arms. She needed to free its contents but she wasn't sure what would happen if she fiddled with the device containing it.

"Give me that!" The speaker was Kurumata, reaching out to grab the bottle. She twisted and kicked, knocking the man down. Then Church was there, telling her, "That thing's too important, Miss Chang. You have to give it to me. National security's on the line."

It seemed ludicrous to Mudan that these people could behave this way with everything going to hell around them. The Black Dragon broke free of Shen's grip in an effort to get at her. Shen caught him again, but not before Raud sent torn up trees and broken stones flying after them in an effort to stop their escape. All the while screaming that the thing Mudan held was his.

When Kurumata tried again, to grab hold of Mudan's prize, she shoved it into Conall's hands and turned on the man, loosing a kick to his chin that sent him stumbling sideways. She'd have pressed the attack but Fukushima was there before she could. "Stand down," the Japanese girl ordered. "We will discuss who owns what when we are no longer in danger of being charred, smashed or, should our ally forget himself, electrocuted."

Chastened, Kurumata set off. The others followed suit, while Conall quietly handed the bottle back to Mudan.

"Your stance was weak, daughter. He should have gone down from that kick."

"This is not the time, father. Let's go." Refusing to argue further, Mudan followed the others, dodging stones and streams of fire as she ran.

《《《

They reached the plane quickly after Mudan 'persuaded' the others to stop wasting time. Fukushima made a mental note to never make Mudan angry with her. She also made a note to find time for a sparring match. Given they survived this madness.

Once inside the plane, Kurumata complained, "Where are we going to go? We should wait for the soldiers to get here."

"I wondered if that was part of your plan," Murtagh said suddenly. "Well, boy, I don't doubt you, or Shikawa, rather, ordered a troop up to deal with the General. But even if they get here in time, they're not going to be much good against a pair of dragons, are they?"

"Even if they aren't," Kurumata snapped, "No one can fly a plane in this weather."

"I can. I'm the best pilot in China," Zhanchi assured him, grinning as he headed for the cockpit. "Now strap yourselves in. This is going to be a wild ride."

They all sat down, Kurumata staring after the pilot with an expression Fukushima didn't like. Then, just as he was about to pull the belt around his waist, he stood up, shouting, "That's who he is! He's that bastard who attacked *Tōgō* Unit!"

Realizing Zhanchi's cocky behavior, combined with his obvious flying skill, had finally made Kurumata remember where he'd seen the pilot before, Fukushima tried to stall him. "Sit down. This isn't the time to argue. We need him to fly the plane." Already they were racing up the runway.

"No. I swore I'd kill that bastard and I'm going to kill him!"

It was typical of the man that he'd entirely ignore his own safety in favor of getting revenge. As Kurumata drew his gun and the plane left the ground, Fukushima made up her mind. She snapped her hand sideways, in a single strike just behind his ear. It was a perfectly aimed, perfectly timed, knockout blow. One her *sensei* would have been proud of.

"Remind me to find time for sparring," Mudan said suddenly, echoing Fukushima's own thoughts. She seemed to realize it, too, and grinned suddenly at her. "If nothing else, we can do with the quiet."

As the plane rocked in the winds of the storm and a stream of flame lit up the night outside, Fukushima thought quiet was the last thing they were going to get.

((((

Mudan watched Conall gaze out the window with rapt attention and wished she didn't have to interrupt him. He looked so delighted with what he was seeing. No doubt he was contemplating the possibilities of creating a tableau based on the fight, or wondering if he could harness the power of a Chinese dragon's lightning—give Shen was willing to cooperate. Still, this was important.

"Conall."

He smiled at her and she felt herself light up at the sight. "What is it?"

"I want to open the bottle."

"Are you out of your mind, girl? You don't even know what that stuff is. None of us do." Lord William sounded panicked, and no blame to him considering they were riding through a storm with two dragons battling furiously around them. "You heard what that man said about it."

Conall looked at the silver metal, then at the bracelet on Mudan's wrist. "She's right, Lord William." He examined the machine atop the jar and fiddled with it thoughtfully. "I need something sharp."

"Here." Mr. Chang handed him a long thin dagger. "Try not to dull the blade if you can help it."

"I'll try, sir."

It took some fiddling but at long last Conall slid the device locking the lid down free. The electricity it emitted obviously shocked him several times in the process, but he ignored it the way he ignored anything that didn't suit him. He worked on the lid now, and Mudan held her breath, wondering if they'd have to break the thing open.

Then the seal snapped and the lid came off. For a moment there was complete quiet and Mudan was about to ask her bracelet what to do. Then, without warning, the contents of the bottle burst free in a swirling storm of small dragon shapes, scattering through the cabin. The other passengers crouched and Lord William shouted, "What the devil are they?"

"Living metal, remember?" Mudan called back, catching hold of one of the little dragons and holding it up. "Come here. Stop that. Child of Dream, help me."

Her bracelet shifted and moved, wrapping itself around the other dragon shape and absorbing it. Surprisingly, it didn't seem any bigger, but something told her it was stronger. "Good little Meng," she told it. "Good baby."

"It's not a pet!" Murtagh complained.

"I'm not so sure," Church said slowly. "That fellow did say something about it having a mind of its own. Miss Chang, you obviously have a rapport with it. Do you think you could get them to calm down? And, while you're at it, make them stop trying to crawl up my pants leg?"

Mudan sighed. It seemed even scattered and not completely itself, Meng had a peculiar and coarse sense of humor.

ᘓᘓᘓ

" AS THE PLANE ROCKED IN THE WINDS
OF THE STORM AND A STREAM OF FLAME
LIT UP THE NIGHT OUTSIDE..."

Conall would have helped gather the bits and pieces of living metal, but it only listened to Mudan. The best he could do was help her find the things: a prospect made more difficult by the fact that the plane kept shifting and tilting. "Zhanchi!" Mudan called at one point. "Can you please fly this plane more level? I am trying to concentrate back here."

"We're flying between two dragons, one of whom is breathing fire and the other of whom is creating a storm to end all storms. No. I cannot fly any more level than I already am." Zhanchi's answer came at the same moment the plane bounced Conall off his feet and dropped him into Mr. Chang's lap.

"Sorry, sir."

"No apologies are necessary, son-in-law to be. I do not ask you to break the laws of gravity."

Reflecting that he probably could, with the right equipment, Conall went back to searching for the little dragons. At last they found them all and while Mudan's bracelet didn't look any different, she thought it was finally whole. "Lord William," she said. "I do not think you, or anyone, can use this for an engine."

"But that's what Soong and his gang were selling it for," Murtagh protested. "They obviously thought it could be used that way."

Thoughtfully, Conall examined the bracelet, contemplating what he'd seen it do so far. "It's aware, right? It understands what you tell it to do?"

"Yes. It does." Mudan looked at it and murmured something in Chinese, too quickly for Conall to follow. Immediately, the little bracelet shifted shape, becoming a sphere covered in fine engravings, then a vase, then a dragon again, this time larger. It sat on Mudan's shoulder with an expression that said it'd found its home, whether or not anyone else agreed.

Conall had a germ of an idea. The question was, was it a good one and would it help them escape? He turned to Mudan, "Dear, am I right in thinking Shen can't fight that other dragon with all his strength because there are people who'd be hurt?" It wouldn't be just them, either. All of Hanchow lay in the path of the battle.

"I believe that is likely to be the problem."

"And that dragon—Raud, wasn't it?—is hunting us because he wants this."

"You are not sending it out to be hunted," Mudan snapped.

Conall smiled and gave the little dragon a pat on its snout as it snorted at him. "No. But Raud will hunt us, if we fly out over sea."

Zhanchi demanded, "Are you out of your mind? We'll be sitting ducks."

"Not if we can put on a burst of speed back to land. Then Sir Bruce... Raud... will be the sitting duck."

Zhanchi went silent. "You think that thing of Mudan's can do that for us?"

"Can you?" Conall asked the little dragon. "They used you to make a normal engine run faster and more efficiently. Can you do it of your own free will? We need to fly out to sea, then very quickly back."

Very slowly, very thoughtfully, the dragon looked at Mudan, who asked in turn, "I would appreciate it if you would, but I do not demand it, if it would cause you harm."

After another breathless moment, it suddenly swarmed up Mudan's arm, licked her cheek in a kiss and raced down and forward. In a second it was gone and the plane's engine suddenly sounded strangely quiet. "I think that was 'yes'," Mudan said softly.

⟪⟪⟪

The change in the engine made flying strangely easy and Zhanchi wished that bracelet of Mudan's was his instead. That was a vain hope and he set it aside in favor of keeping as level as he could. He could feel the winds buffeting the plane, could hear the screams of the two dragons as they fought and hoped Shen would understand the plan when they reached open water.

"McLeod, help me," he called. The ease of flight went only so far. He needed someone to keep an eye on the gauges, to tell him where he was and to keep him properly oriented. One mistake and they might crash into the China Sea to never be seen again.

Sitting in the co-pilot's seat, McLeod did as Zhanchi ordered. He also helped steady the plane as the winds tried to take it out of Zhanchi's hands. Feeling a grudging respect for the man, Zhanchi still snapped orders sharply as he banked and turned. The Black Dragon seemed to realize what he was up to and began trying to drive him back. He knew, Zhanchi guessed, that Shen was more than his match if he used his full power.

Behind him, Zhanchi heard someone throwing up and called back, "There are airsick bags in storage. Use them!" At the same time he dodged the plane downwards, side-slipping and evading the dragon before it catch hold of them.

Over and over they twisted, turned and moved. Over and over the Black Dragon tried to block him and the Flowering Dragon protected. At last they reached open water and Zhanchi said, "Mudan, tell your pet to kick it into high gear. I'm going to make for the mainland. Right now."

The plane screamed around them as it rushed through the air. Wind set them rocking momentarily, then there were no winds strong enough to match their speed. Zhanchi fought to keep control, feeling the rudders fight him. Behind them, something seemed to explode in the sky, a huge blast of purple-blue light that resembled nothing so much as the most splendid firework ever.

Wishing he could stay to watch and confident that the Flowering Dragon would defeat his enemy, Zhanchi focused on getting his plane home and in one piece. They were moving so fast the wings were beginning to shudder. They couldn't take this kind of force for long, he realized. An engine this strong, with speeds this great, was far more than any plane had been designed for. He yelled, "Slow down! We can slow down now!"

Even as the engine quieted, even as the winds rushing past slowed, Zhanchi felt the shaking that heralded an imminent breakdown. There was no choice. He had to get this bird landed and he had to do it fast. Spotting a field below him, a shadow sharply limned by the full moon's light, he turned for it. It was short, the shortest runway he'd ever landed on, but it was their only hope.

"Are you out of your mind?" Murtagh shouted, seeing where Zhanchi was headed. "You can't land there."

"If we don't land there, we don't land anywhere," Zhanchi shouted back. "Hold tight and pray!" He reset the flaps, adjusting his speed and prayed to Lunghua for protection. He just hoped Shen wasn't too busy to hear him.

Then the wheels touched down. Bounced once. Bounced twice. Bounced a third and final time before staying down. Zhanchi hit the brakes, screaming at the engine, or the thing driving it, to stop.

It heard him and it listened. Between that and his brakes, and despite the inertia trying to drive them forward, the plane slowed and finally halted, a faint purple mist dissipating as the plane went still.

At last, shaking and ready to faint, Zhanchi turned off the engine and released the controls. Then, with a cocky smile that he only partly felt, he climbed out of his seat and told his passengers, "Thank you for flying Metal Dragon Airlines. I trust you've enjoyed your flight. Please watch your step when leaving the aircraft."

Murtagh stared at him. "You... did it."

"Of course I did," Zhanchi said, grinning broadly. "I told you before, sir. I'm the best pilot in China."

Chapter Twenty-One
Transportation Facilities to any Other Place are Readily Available

Fukushima watched Kurumata in his hospital bed. He wasn't badly injured but her strike had had the convenient side-effect of confusing his memories. Somehow he thought he was still assigned to *Tōgō* Unit, and he was bewildered by the presence of British nurses and doctors. He kept demanding to know how they'd gotten into Manchuria. No matter how many times they explained he was in Shanghai, he simply couldn't wrap his mind around the fact.

"Poor man. He never was very stable." Shikawa eyed Fukushima from the doorway and shook his head sadly. "You did right, stopping him from using the Soong device while you were in the air."

Fukushima bowed. "It would have been fatal for all of us. Mr. McLeod believes it was never intended to drive any sort of engine. That it was too dangerous for any but the most experienced to handle." That was the truth, as far as it went.

"Just as well it dissipated, then. I wonder if Soong had any clue what he was dealing with." Shikawa turned to leave. "Speaking of whom, have you heard what happened to his lieutenant?"

"Feng Wugong? He hasn't been seen since the fight. Our soldiers, those not killed in the storm or by the traps surrounding *Chinglung* Castle, say the only ones left there were a few dozen children and women. It appears Zhao's daughter is doing what she can to take care of things, but she's just one woman. She won't be able to control her father's men."

"Good. The General might have been an actual threat in the future." Shikawa smiled. "What of the pilot, the one who got you back home safely? What are the chances of his being a problem for us? I understand he's Feng Wugong's brother?"

Fukushima followed Shikawa outside. "Feng Zhanchi has nothing to do with Wugong's gang. As near as I can tell, the only thing that matters to him is flight. Not that he's ever likely to amount to much with the CNAC. I have a feeling they're going to be annoyed with him over that plane."

"Pity he isn't Japanese. We could use him when our time comes." Shikawa smiled, taking a deep breath of air as he surveyed Shanghai's busy streets. "And it is coming, my dear girl. It is coming."

⟨⟨⟨

Bai She walked up behind the young man standing alongside the Whangpoo River. He could tell Zhanchi was fretting and understood why. It was the nature of humans to doubt, a thing the youngest of Khaitan's Immortals would have to learn to inure himself to.

Taking pity on both Zhanchi and Shen, he told the human. "Faith in one's God requires belief that they'll be there for you."

The boy had been so focused on the water that he nearly fell in when Bai She spoke. He turned and bowed respectfully, "Sir." Then a startled note entered his voice and he added, "One's God?" The truth was clearly dawning on him, though, and in a most satisfactory way. At least some of those outside Khaitan still understood the nature of Gods. Still understood that the Gods didn't need belief to live but for other reasons entirely. Faith acted as the lightning rod that allowed Gods to act upon the world. Without it, a God could do little. There was nothing more frustrated than a God without followers. "I'm no priest."

"Shen Lunghua's too young for a priest. He's just a little over a thousand years old. But even baby Immortals need someone to have faith in them. Be sure he'll come back and he will." Bai She's shadows roamed around him, poking curious noses into everything and startling those observant enough to notice. Fortunately, they were far enough away from the city that there weren't many.

"I was hoping he'd come back to the temple," Zhanchi said, and Bai She's shadows showed him pointing away from the river, towards the tall pagoda that marked the site.

"Hope is close to faith, but not the same thing," Bai She pointed out gently. "Where there's hope, there's doubt."

Zhanchi took a deep breath and Bai She knew he was calming himself. He heard the slowing of the boy's pulse, the quieting of his breath and, slowly felt the surge of much needed certainty. That same belief in Shen had given the young dragon the power he needed to change and now it gave him the connection he needed to return.

Suddenly the water erupted in a geyser in front of them and splashed both Zhanchi and Bai She. "Oh, thank you, nephew. I needed a bath," Bai She said sharply. "Especially with that river's water."

Transforming to human form once more and ignoring the reactions of those who'd seen his arrival, Shen said, "You're welcome, younger uncle."

"That was sarcasm, boy. Learn it."

"I know." They smiled at each other with what Bai She knew were near identically arrogant smiles. Shen was the child of the Old Man of the East—the youngest son of one of Khaitan's first Gods—but the boy had spent a great deal of time exploring the waters in Bai She's realm below the land. He couldn't help picking up some of Bai She's personality.

"Sir? Are you all right?" Zhanchi interrupted their reunion. "Is there something you want me to do?"

Shen considered the boy and Bai She said, warningly, "He's still needed here. And now that the thing we came for is safe, we are not permitted to remain."

That made both youths turn to him, protesting. Zhanchi because Shen had promised flight and would surely deliver and Shen because he'd promised flight and must deliver. "He's my one true worshipper," Shen said. "How can I leave him to his fate?"

"You and he will always be connected. If he needs your presence, you'll know and nothing in the world will keep you from going to him. But right now, this land is on the precipice and as far as I can tell, nothing will pull it back. China will need its greatest pilot all too soon."

((((

Zhi Lin watched her soldiers clean up the mess with a sharp eye for any mistakes. To tell the truth, it wasn't so bad. The stairs and trees leading down to the airfield were broken and shattered where the dragons had passed, there was a great big hole at the top of the wall around the courtyard and a fair number of fire and lightning scorch marks all over the place. Oh, yes, and blood staining the pavement where the Black Dragon had bitten her father's head clean off.

It surprised her only a little to find she wasn't sorry. She hadn't loved Zhao. No one actually loved Zhao. But she had been his loyal child for so long that she would have expected the shock of his death to make her yearn for revenge. Not that she could get it. The other dragon, the one with gold, green and purple scales, had done the job for her. She'd watched the fight through Third Wife's scry glass, with every other member of the household. When Lunghua had wrapped himself entirely around Zhao's killer and let loose a coruscating lightshow that ended only when Raud dropped lifeless into the Chinese Sea, they'd all cheered.

If her brother were anything but a fool, Zhi Lin would have had no chance to take over after her father. He might be younger than she, but he was a boy. He was also far too foolish and childlike for any of Zhao's men to follow willingly. If the family was to survive, someone strong had to do the job and she was the strongest of Zhao's children.

"I could use a good thief and sneak," she told the man sitting on the steps munching a chicken leg with obvious enjoyment. "Are you sure you won't stay?"

"I have an allergy to real work," Chen answered. "Sets off my coughing something awful." He wiped his hands and mouth. "But I can be hired if I like the job."

Before she could argue, he rose to his feet and started down the steps, only to stop and look up at her thoughtfully. "There's trouble coming to China and things are going to get rough, Zhi Lin. You don't have to be your father's daughter in every respect."

"How do you mean?"

"Zhao Zhu wanted power. He wanted to be Emperor. Speaking from experience, the job's not worth the effort. There's always someone waiting in the wings to stab you in the back and take over. Find what you want to protect and protect it. Sometimes, that's about the best anyone can do."

"What do you suggest?"

Chen shrugged. "Well, you've one hell of a talent in the kitchen. And Chinese cuisine's getting popular. You could always start a cooking school." His smile turned dangerous as he added, "And you might find a use for your other skills in the very near future."

◖◖◖

Zhanchi returned to Lunghua airport because he had nowhere else to go. Shen and Bai She had left, drawn through Bai She's shadows back to Khaitan. He still had a feeling of being the center of Shen's regard, but that wasn't going to feed or clothe him. With Murtagh's plans gone up in smoke, or absorbed into that pretty little bracelet Mudan wore, the only thing Zhanchi could do was go back to work.

He was helping out in the hangar, fixing the plane he'd landed and ignoring the maintenance crew's complaints over what he'd done to it when Murtagh suddenly spoke behind him. "And what do you think you're doing?"

When Zhanchi turned, startled, he realized it wasn't just Murtagh. McLeod's boss, Striker was with him, and, surprisingly enough, Mudan's father. He might expect the first two to be working together, still, but how did Mr. Chang come into it? "Sir?"

"I seem to remember hiring you for the duration."

Somehow, Zhanchi managed not to snap that Murtagh had hired him to fly, not drive. Instead he said, "I believe the engine I was to help test isn't available anymore."

"That doesn't mean you're not needed," Striker said. "That engine isn't any use, but McLeod says he has some ideas on the subject."

Slowly realizing what that might mean, Zhanchi asked, "You're going to build planes?"

"We're going to build plane engines and you're going to help test them." Murtagh eyed him sharply. "You're the best pilot in China, after all, and we need the best."

Zhanchi couldn't argue with that. "What of Mr. Chang?" he asked. That worthy had been standing, smiling genially, off to the side and allowing the two Westerners to do all the talking.

Before either Striker or Murtagh could open their mouths, Mr. Chang chuckled. "McLeod is about to become my son-in-law. Being the filial child that he is, he is providing his services to the British-Oriental Consortium through the auspices of Jeen Loon Enterprises. I too," Mr. Chang said, sounding terribly pleased with himself, "have always wanted wings."

Zhanchi's distant uncle, Feng Ru had died testing his engines, but he had died doing the thing he loved most. Reflecting that the choice between being constantly sidelined in the CNAC aerodrome and taking admitted risks with untried engines, was an easy one to make, Zhanchi found a rag and cleaned off his hand before offering it to Mr. Chang. "Then I will be glad to help provide them, sir."

《《《

Incense rose around Mudan as she sat in the shrine inside her father's Shanghai house. Somewhere outside she could hear the sounds of people talking excitedly. But she wasn't part of all that. All she could do, all she was allowed to do, was sit here and contemplate the slightly daft face of her more than slightly daft God.

She couldn't even perform as a Priestess. Not right now. Another woman, her cousin Tan's mother, Chiang, was handling that duty. Even now she was dancing and singing around the room, her face slowly taking on the bewildered look of one lost in delirium.

Some priestesses enjoyed the state a bit too much, forgetting how easy it was to get lost in and easier still to misunderstand what they were being told. Fortunately, Chiang wasn't one of those sorts. She maintained her Self beneath their God's touch with a will that matched, and possibly overmatched Mudan's own.

The bells and chimes grew louder, while the smell of roast pig and lard cakes rose from the platter in front of her. Both were the God's favorites and were intended for him, but Mudan couldn't help her stomach growling at the scent. She'd been sitting here all night in vigil, waiting for this moment.

At last it, and he, came. Not the God, for he was always there, but Conall. Dressed in red like Mudan, he looked almost as bewildered as Chiang, though for different reasons.

They'd barely returned from their dealings with Zhao and that wild flight, to find the entire family preparing for the ceremony that would tie their fates together. Most Chinese took their time with marriages, but the Jeen Loon, who all too often had no time to waste on fripperies like matchmakers and fortune-telling, didn't wait. Once a couple had agreed to wed and their marriage had been approved, it happened.

The young men who'd helped Conall dress handed him off to her father, who looked him over carefully, as if he were buying an antique of particularly uncertain antecedence. Then, with a single nod, Mudan's father led Conall forward and made him kneel beside her. "I allow," was all he said.

Immediately the Priestess began to speak. It was the God's usual confused babble. This being a wedding, Meng Huang Hsiang didn't need to offer much in the way of advice. So while he would say what was on his mind, it seldom made much sense.

"The old times and the new times entwine. The Golden Dragon's heirs rise from the earth and from metal to battle those who would harm their blood. The eagle and the shining one join together to produce a bright star and fire spawned from the pit of hell itself rises and aspires to become a God."

Although Mudan knew the God's promises usually came true, she also knew it did no good to try to understand them. Instead she bowed her head, waiting for his blessing. It came soon, the Priestess' hands hot on Mudan's forehead and Conall's. With great effort the God said clearly, "You are much loved and I am much pleased. You may not wed by man's law yet. Blood will spill and bombs will fall, but I promise you, that day will come."

Then they were wed, at least by her family's rules, and the noise and excitement was almost enough to make Mudan wish they'd eloped.

))((

The *Empress of China* was once more steaming its way across the Pacific Ocean, this time from north to south, headed for Taiwan. From there, Conall and Mudan would catch another of the line's ships on a grand tour that would take them all the way round the Pacific Rim before returning to San Francisco and finally Strikersport. They'd be gone for over a month, ample time to provide Mr. Chang with grandchildren, if they were so inclined.

"Not that I'm in any sort of rush," Conall admitted as he watched the coast of China recede. "It's going to take some time to get people accustomed to our being together."

Mudan smiled with that serene expression. "It is a thing a father must say," she told Conall. "He does not expect us to hurry either. Besides, there is much that we must do beforehand."

That was all too true. Conall had seen bits and pieces of the situation in Shanghai. Although he could be fairly accused of being distractible and unaware of social nuances, it'd been impossible to miss the little aggressions, the frictions and the general contempt that concealed itself beneath the apparently exuberant and pleasure-loving society.

To his mind, Shanghai was a microcosm of the Far East, with all the Western influences trying to remake it according to their point of view, the Chinese effort to passively ignore what they could not, yet, drive out and the Japanese desire to take the reins from the West and make all Asia its own. He couldn't say who was going to win in the end but he was very much afraid of what was coming. And now that he was, by marriage, a member of the Jeen Loon, it behooved him to be concerned about its interests and those of his family.

In the meantime, though, an all too brief interlude with his wife would not go amiss. His wife. He loved that word and yearned to shout it to everyone, despite law and custom. One day he would, he promised himself.

He'd be fighting for that the same way he'd fought for her hand. Silently, he drew her close.

"What is that poking me?" Mudan asked suddenly. Before he could stop her, she pulled the guidebook he'd carried all this time out of his coat pocket. "This thing, still?"

"It was interesting," he said, a little weakly.

"Perhaps, but you no longer need it." She started to lift it over the rail then saw the look on his face. Indulgently, she smiled. "Well, keep it then. But please, for the love of Meng Huang Hsiang and all the Gods, don't read that part about cabarets again."

Putting the book away, Conall said obediently, stuffing the book back into his pocket, "I promise. Never again." Then he kissed her and didn't care who aboard might see.

The End

About Our Creators

Author

BARBARA DORAN—has been making up stories for as long as she can remember. From playing Ms. Marvel to her best friend's Captain Marvel to writing new stories for old characters (Hannibal King, X-Men, Green Hornet, The Saint, The Shadow and many others), to writing gaming and anime fanfiction online.

After ten years behind the keyboard as a software engineer, Barbara realized that her true love wasn't coding but making stuff up. So when she left that career in favor of dealing with two frequent interruptions of her life (namely her own personal Tiger and Dragon), she decided to use what little time they allowed her to work on writing. Her Long Suffering Husband, without whom she could never have managed such a goal, has been nothing if not supportive.

Along with reading every mystery, SF and fantasy book she could get her hands on, Barbara grew up watching Star Trek, Batman, Green Hornet, along with the usual Saturday morning cartoons. She became addicted to shows like Battle of the Planets and Doctor Who in her teens and discovered Run Run Shaw's martial arts flicks some years later. Those influences, along with a love of folklore and mythology, have become part of the world some small portion of her mind lives in. When, of course, she isn't chasing Tiger and Dragon from one school event to another.

Barbara can be contacted at BarbaraDoran@sumergoscriptum.com. Her website is http://www.sumergoscriptum.com/barbaradoran/.

Interior Illustrator

GARY KATO—was born in Honolulu, Hawaii in 1949. He graduated from the University of Hawaii with a Bachelor of Fine Arts degree. His comic book work has appeared in such varied titles as DESTROYER DUCK, THUNDERBUNNY, MS. TREE and MR. JIGSAW. He's also illustrated children's books such as THE MENEHUNE OF NAUPAKA VILLAGE, and the currently available BARRY BASKERVILLE SOLVES A CASE, BARRY BASKERVILLE RETURNS, BARRY BASKERVILLE'S BLUE BICYCLE and JAMIE AND THE FISH-EYED GOGGLES. He's also been a contributor to the Children's Television Workshop magazines, 3-2-1 CONTACT and KID CITY.

Cover Artist

ROB DAVIS - began his professional art career doing illustrations for role-playing games in the late 1980s. Not long after he began lettering and inking, then penciling comics for a number of small black and white comics publishers- most notably for Eternity Comics, which eventually became Malibu Comics in the 1990s, on their book SCIMIDAR with writer R.A. Jones. Branching out to other black and white publishers and eventually working at both DC and Marvel Rob worked on likeness intensive comics like TV adaptations of QUANTUM LEAP and STAR TREK's many incarnations mostly on the DEEP SPACE NINE comics for Malibu. At Marvel he worked on the Saturday morning cartoon adaptation PIRATES OF DARK WATER.

After the comics industry implosion in the late 1990's Rob picked up work on video games, advertising illustration and T-shirt design as well as some small press comics like ROBYN OF SHERWOOD for Caliber. Rob continues to do the occasional self-published comic book as well as publisher and designer for his small-press production REDBUD STUDIO COMICS. Rob is Art Director, Designer and Illustrator for the New Pulp production outfit AIRSHIP 27 partnered with writer/editor Ron Fortier. Rob is the recipient of the PULP FACTORY AWARD for "Best Interior Illustrations" in 2010 and 2015 for his work on SHERLOCK HOLMES: CONSULTING DETECTIVE and has been nominated for the same award every year since the award's inception. He works and lives in central Missouri with his wife and two children.

Trouble in Strikersport

When a mysterious evil force known only as the Voice begins to take control of the local mobs in the coast city of Strikersport, two new heroes appear on the scene. Their origin, the neighborhood streets of Chinatown. The masked Tiger and Dragon wield both science and magic in their battle to combat the forces of darkness. Soon several of the city's prominent citizens become players in this cataclysmic war. These include players from a wealthy family with roots to Strikersport history, a rookie cop and a crusading newspaper editor.

Writer Barbara Doran spins a classic pulp adventure with breakneck pacing, original characters and a tangled plot that will keep readers guessing to the very end. Mixing martial arts with Chinese mysticism, she offers a truly unique action mystery sure to entertain readers from beginning to end.

AN AIRSHIP 27 PRODUCTION

NEW **PULP**

PULP FICTION FOR A NEW GENERATION!
FOR AVAILABILITY: AIRSHIP27HANGAR.COM

www.ingramcontent.com/pod-product-compliance
Lightning Source LLC
Chambersburg PA
CBHW051142260626
47170CB00005B/1929